THE UNEXPECTED QUEST

Kathleen Bushell-Partridge

ISBN: 9798793192514

DEDICATION

Inspired by my Grandson Jamie Bushell

MAIN CHARACTERS

Daniel

Parents: Dad – Arthur - Mum – Jean

Axel

Parents: Dad – Tobias (Toby) - Mum – Analisa

Roman

Parents - Dad – Stefan - Mum Selina

Summer

Parents - Dad – Jed - Mum – Rebecca

Old Man - Professor

ADDITIONAL CHARACTERS

Jethro - Young man that befriended the children

Mombo – Doctor

Jack - At the Newsprint office

Jane - At the newsprint office

Lieutenant Green - Miami Detective Agency?

Detective Brown - Miami Detective Agency?

Tom - Friend of Jethro

Mombos wife

CONTENTS

1: AN UNEXPECTED SURPRISE

Told by Daniel

It's another dreary day with rain pouring down, as it's not uncommon in England, in the 1980s, whatever the season, and today, things just don't feel right. I have no real reason for it; some may even say I am ungrateful. I'm not, it's just it doesn't sit right with me. Sorry, I shouldn't burden you with my troubles, after all you're a complete stranger. It's just that it's not like me to be down or moody. I'm usually quite a cheerful guy that meets challenges head on without worrying about the consequences.

I'm sorry, we have not been introduced, my name is Daniel and I live near London, England.

You probably don't have a clue of what I am talking about. Well, it's like this…

I've never been on holiday before. I mean a real holiday. Of course, I've been camping with the Scouts many times - I expect you have heard of the organisation - and I have also been to stay with friends for a week or two at a time. It's been great fun.

Well, I suppose I was expecting to do the same this summer. At least that is what I think we were all expecting until a few weeks ago.

Oh dear! I am going to sound ungrateful. You won't think much of me when I tell you. It was so unexpected you see, not the sort of thing my mother would normally do. Even my Dad was stunned until she explained.

You see, Mum's been working extra hard since Xmas, long hours, extra to her normal hours. They call it overtime. Well, she has been pretty tired and a bit ratty, which she isn't normally. Come to that none of us are normally, so it was a bit out of character all round when she dropped the bombshell.

Here goes, you will now think I'm mad or ungrateful or just plain stupid. Although it wasn't my first reaction, that was the problem, just the subsequent one.

We were all sitting at the table eating dinner when she said, "Hey guys can I have your attention for a minute?" Dad and I looked at each other thinking this is odd. Then Dad said, "Sure love, what's up?

"Well, you have both been great helping me out whilst I've been working overtime, so when I got my pay cheque, I found it was a pretty good amount extra, so I thought I would do something to say thank you."

"That's very kind of you love, but we don't need to be thanked, we didn't mind helping you out, did we Daniel?"

"Err, no Dad."

"Oh, that's nice of you both but you don't understand. I've already done it."

"Done what love?"

"Booked a holiday."

"You have, have you, where to love?

"Miami"

"What! You're not serious, are you?"

"Yes, love I'm very serious. I've booked it in the school summer holidays so that the three of us can go."

"Wow that's great Mum!"

"Thanks Daniel. It will be your first big holiday. You get to go on a plane for eight hours or so. It will be great fun and a great experience."

"What! Eight hours? You must be joking, that doesn't sound like fun to me. I'm not sure about this idea Mum. It doesn't feel right. It sounds great, but I get a funny feeling about it."

"Don't worry Daniel, I understand. It's just the shock."

"If you say so Mum, I'm not so sure."

"Well, it's a few weeks away, so there's plenty of time to get used to the idea, after all it's a holiday of a lifetime."

"Thank you darling it was very thoughtful of you, and you deserve it after all that hard work."

"Yes Mum, Dad's right, I'm sorry. I guess my friends will be bowled over when I tell them!"

"I guess they will son. Now let's finish our meal and we can discuss the details later."

That was how it was left, we finished dinner and Mum and Dad sat talking until bedtime. I went off to my room to finish my homework to try to forget what Mum had said.

So, do you see what I'm saying, I sound ungrateful don't I? I feel it myself so I can't blame you if you think so too.

Dad and I talked about it many times over the next few weeks. I explained my lack of enthusiasm to him. I just had a bad feeling that something would go wrong. I wanted the holiday, but couldn't shift the feeling. Silly I know, but that was me, always cautious when my sixth sense kicks in.

Anyway, the weeks went by with no mishap and the holiday is due to start.

All my friends have gone on their holidays, envious of me, as they are not going abroad. So, I need to buck up my ideas and be more grateful. After all, who else would want to stay here for a holiday. It hasn't stopped raining for days. Maybe Mum's right, perhaps it was the shock of her doing something so spontaneous, with not having time beforehand to have discussed it, and got used to the idea. I guess I'll never know.

Well, whoever you are, thanks for listening, I'll let you know how it goes.

"Daniel are you ready? If we don't hurry, we will miss the plane. Your mother has finished the packing and she's in a hurry to leave."

"I'm coming Dad, although I'd rather stay here. Can't you and Mum go on holiday without me? I don't mean to sound ungrateful, but it's not much fun going on holiday with your parents and leaving all your friends behind. What am I supposed to do whilst you and Mum go around all the galleries and sit sunbathing on the beach?"

"Look son, we have been through this numerous times already. We are not leaving you behind. Sure, it's a long flight, but you can watch films on planes these days and walk around, besides you may meet some kids your own age and have a good time. This is your first big holiday, which me and your, Mum have worked hard to get. Surely it wouldn't be too much to ask for you to come along without a fuss. "

"I'm sorry Dad, but it doesn't feel right, I can't help it, I'm sure it's going to end in trouble. I just feel it. Call it a sixth sense or something."

"Look lad, it's just nerves because you have never been on a plane before. It will be fine. Your Mum would have made all the arrangements so that there are no problems with the journey or booking. You know what she's like. She will have everything down to a fine detail with all the I's dotted and T's crossed".

"Arthur, are you and Daniel ready? The taxi's here."

"We are just coming love, aren't we Daniel?"

I looked at my father with a pleading look in my eyes.

Then with a heavy sigh," Yes! Mum we're coming, we wouldn't miss it for the world."

I grimaced at Dad, who showed his gratitude by grinning back.

We piled the luggage into the taxi, then waved goodbye to the house and neighbours who wished us a happy holiday.

"Three weeks in the sun, what could be better Arthur? You and Daniel can explore Miami whilst I sunbathe. What fun eh?"

"Yes love, it sounds great doesn't it, Daniel?"

"Oh sure, just great Mum."

And that's how it was, at least on the take-off, flight and landing.

Hang around if you want to know more.

2: I KNEW THIS WASNT A GOOD IDEA

I told them it would end in trouble, but they didn't listen to me, no one ever did. I was the runt of the litter so as to speak, no I wasn't an animal, but I was the smallest of the three of us and the weakest, physically that is, so they called me a runt. Just like when a puppy is born into a litter and not expected to survive, as very little and weak compared to its siblings. That's a grown-up word for brothers and sisters. My parents are always saying it, so I asked them what it meant.

I haven't got any by the way, brothers and sisters that is. They just had me and weren't too impressed when I arrived, so didn't bother to have any more. At least that is what they tell people who say how unlucky they are to only have the one, as they have three or four. I think secretly my parents are glad they only have one, as some of their friends' children are a bit of a handful.

Well, that's enough about me for the moment, I must stop feeling sorry for myself. As I was saying, before I started talking about myself.

I had warned them it would get us into trouble. No silly, not my parents, although I did say I had a bad feeling about the holiday.

I don't however mean them. I mean my new friends. Oh, sorry I haven't told you about them yet have I.

Well, they are great. We've only known each other a few days but get on like a house on fire, not that we're much alike. Especially as one of them is a girl, that's Summer. She's pretty, but pretty-strange too, because she likes hanging out with boys. Summer is not a bit girly as she's game for anything that's adventurous, or dangerous. She will always jump in first if there's a fight. She's thirteen, but got very long legs, tall for her age and skinny like us boys. If it wasn't for her long blonde hair, you might mistake her for one. She's a bit bossy too, unlike Roman my other friend.

He's thirteen too, but he's much calmer and quieter than Summer. He's game for adventure, but more cautious, and always tells us to hold back. He likes to think things through a lot before doing things. Summer's always saying he will miss all the fun if he doesn't hurry up. He can be a bit reckless at times though, when his temper is up. Then there is no stopping him. He'll ignore anything you say and jump in with both feet. I like him though, he's got a great laugh, brilliant sense of humour, you know the type, I'm sure.

Well, enough about them, I think you get the picture; maybe I should explain that Roman is his name not his country, except he does come from Rome in Italy. Confusing, eh?

He's got thick black hair and glasses and speaks with an accent. I'm British by the way at least that's what I'm told, my parents are Greek though, they said I was born in England which makes me

British. Summer's American in case you hadn't guessed, so we're a motley crew.

Any way I have digressed enough, so back to where we came in. I warned them that it would end in trouble. They wouldn't listen.

It all started when we landed at the airport. We were virtual strangers at the time. We had all been on the planes that had landed that day and were waiting to collect our baggage at the Miami airport. Yes, that's in America. The U.S.A. As it's sometimes, called.

Anyhow, we were queueing up in a long row when this old man with a beard, as long as Summer's hair, came shuffling through shouting, "They have stolen my staff. They have taken my staff. Thieves, robbers they have stolen my staff."

He got himself so upset that he collapsed at my feet. My parents pushed me out of his way but as they did, he grabbed my hands and with his piecing blue eyes staring into me or through me, he pleaded for my help. Well, as you can imagine, all the passengers crowded round, and in them were Roman and Summer.

Most of the people just stood there in shock. I couldn't move as he held onto me so tight. My parents called for an airport security person. Then both Summer and Roman just bundled in and helped. Summer got down on her knees and helped the old man get up whilst Roman spoke gently to him saying, "We will help," whilst looking at me to reinforce what he was saying to the man. I nodded, feeling speechless, as if in some kind of surreal situation.

The security man then appeared and broke up the crowds, shouting, "Collect your baggage, and move away".

He then took the old man by the arm, "Come with me sir" and gently, but firmly led him away. As he was still holding on to me, I was obliged to go with him. Of course, my mother followed, saying to my Dad, "Collect the luggage" as she passed him.

As you can imagine, Summer and Roman came too. We were all bundled into a small office. The security man turning to my mother, "Madam, please explain what has happened".

My mother being a teacher by profession, was used to taking charge and explaining things simply said, "The man came running along the corridor shouting that someone had stolen his staff. Then as if exhausted, he collapsed at my son's feet, and held onto him. I called for security, and the children here, helped to get the man to his feet and calm him."

"Do you know this man?"

"No, we do not know who he is."

"Have you or your son met him before today?"

"No! we had never met him before. Nor do we know who or where his staff are or how many of them, they are. Or what he means by staff. You will have to speak to him about that."

"Thank you, Madam, I shall do just that."

Then turning to the old man, "Explain yourself."

The old man, each time he was asked, kept replying, "They have stolen my staff, no, I don't know who," turning to me saying each time over and over again, "Please help me."

So, all I could say was "Yes."

The frustrated security man, having all the information he could gain, turned to the old man saying, "Let go of his hand." Then turning to me said "Please leave the room," and to my mother, "You also." Then turning back to the old man, "You remain with me."

We did as he requested.

As I left, I could still feel the old man's eyes boring into me. His voice was calling for me to help him. I turned and smiled at him and nodded. As I did so, I felt a strange connection to him. I knew that I had met him somewhere in the past and would meet him again somewhere in the future,

It was strange, as I had no recollection of him, as far as I knew he was a total stranger to me.

I shrugged off the feeling as best as I could and went with my mother to meet my Dad and help with the luggage. The others also went off to find their families then leave the airport for their intended destinations.

Well, I thought that was the end of the day's excitement and thought no more about it whilst I helped my parents load the taxi and travel to the hotel. How wrong I was? Would you believe it? I walked into the entrance foyer and guess who was standing there.

You wouldn't believe it! I know I couldn't, at least not at first. The man with the long beard was standing at the desk demanding a room.

The receptionist looked fraught or stressed, trying to explain that they were fully booked and that he would have to try elsewhere. The old man was rooted to the spot, insisting that he had booked and was saying, "I am not leaving until I'm meant to, at the end of my vacation."

I tried to hide behind my Dad, so that the man wouldn't see me. My Mum, however, walked up to the reception counter and interrupted him, "Please may I book in and have my room key and a porter to carry the bags?" The old man recognised her at once, and without moving explained to Mum, "The lady is saying the hotel is fully booked! I insist that they have taken my room for someone else!"

"Is this true?"

"No, we are fully booked. This man did not book in advance, we have no rooms left."

"That is a lie. I have my booking form here," and with that he pulled a piece of paper from his pocket and slapped it down on the desk. "I am sorry sir, this is for a different hotel, you have made a mistake, you are booked into the Miami Beach Hotel. This is the Miami hotel, would you like me to call you a taxi, sir, to take you there?"

The old man collapsed again as he realised his mistake. My mother helped him up into a sitting position, whilst I looked on from behind my father. The lady at the desk continued to look flustered.

"Call a taxi for the gentleman," my mother commanded the receptionist. "Then when you have done that, ring the Miami Beach hotel and explain that you are sending him over, and that he has had a stressful day and will need seeing to his room straight away."

"Yes Ma'am, straight away"

"Oh, and when you have done that, call the porter, who after he has seen the gentleman and his luggage into the taxi, can take our luggage to our rooms."

"Why yes ma'am, your key ma'am."

"Arthur, give me a hand here to help the gentleman to his feet."

"Yes dear, straight away dear," and with that I was no longer hidden from the man's view.

His eyes bore into me, compelling me to go to his aid. My father and I went with him to the taxi, assisting him and the porter with his luggage. He continued to say "My staff has been stolen, help me" I reassured him and with my father's permission, agreed to visit him the next day.

Well if that wasn't enough excitement for my first day arrival in Miami, I don't know what is. I can tell you, when I was eventually able to go to my room, I flung myself on my bed. Jet lag took over; I drifted off to sleep, wondering what was going to happen next.

3: MIAMI HOTEL

I awoke late the next morning the sun was streaming in through my window. It was going to be hot and sunny. Even though the room was air conditioned, I could feel its warmth through the glass.

The rattle of cups and saucers drifted through from my parents' room. They had ordered early morning tea, both already up and about, dressed and ready to go down for breakfast.

My mother put her head round the door, "Oh good, you're awake at last, did you sleep well, it's a lovely day and breakfast is in half an hour. Can you put a shift on, your father's hungry and waiting to go down."

Without waiting for a reply, she closed the door again, clear in her mind that I had got the message which I certainly had, as I had learnt a long time ago that if my father was hungry, you made sure he could eat soon, or he was like a bear with a sore head.

I stared at the closed door for a few minutes, a sense of unease, running through my body, without understanding why. I had a feeling that something bad was going to happen, and that I was going to be caught up in the middle of it.

I dragged myself from the bed, showered and dressed. I too

was hungry, though not sure if I could eat with this feeling of anxiety. I was about to open my door, when my fathers' voice called, "Are you ready yet? It's getting late. Don't forget you promised to go and see that old guy yesterday. We need to go straight after breakfast, I've arranged a cab for 10 am."

Pulling the door open I stepped out of the room, "I'm ready Dad."

"Good, let's go."

We left the room and went down in the lift, my stomach churning over, matching the sinking feeling of the lift's movement, down through the different floors.

The dining room was a very large, square, ornate room. It had various white plaster busts of famous people set into alcoves around the room. The walls were blue in colour, and the ceiling was painted with scenes of Greek or Roman battles.

It felt oppressive, even though it was light and airy. There were large round tables, set with white cloths and cutlery, and a small table centrepiece of blue and white flowers. Six or eight ornate chairs were set round each table.

We were shown to a table in the middle of the room, which was packed with people. It was the height of the holiday season, so the hotel was fully booked.

We only required three of the seats at the table, so it wasn't long after we sat down, that the waiter showed three more people to our table.

My parents weren't too pleased about this, but I didn't mind, especially as one of them was a boy of a similar age to me.

"Hello, welcome to the table, my name is Arthur" my father grunted, "And this is my wife Jean and son Daniel."

"Thank you, this is my wife, Annalisa and my son Axel. I am Tobias, Toby for short. We were not expecting to share tables, so I apologise for any inconvenience we may have caused you."

"No, no problem." my father blustered, "Can't be helped, Miami is crowded, so lucky to get a hotel room, let alone a table for breakfast. Think no more about it, let's eat, so we can all get on with our day."

The waiter brought large shiny blue menus and took our orders. "I'll have pancakes with maple syrup, and a coke. What are you having Axel? "

"Oh! I'll have the same please." Our parents ordered pancakes too, but also ordered things on the side like grits, (that's American for small pieces of crisp bacon). They also had coffee and cereals to start, whilst they waited for their breakfast to be cooked.

Axel spoke very little over breakfast. Other than telling me that he was thirteen and there on holiday with his parents, having also arrived yesterday. I gained little information from him.

I therefore looked round at the other tables and was surprised and pleased to see that Summer and Roman were also having breakfast, which meant they were also staying in the hotel. They were sitting at different tables, so I just waved to them, signalling that I would see them later.

"Come on Daniel, eat up, I don't want to keep the taxi waiting."

"Ok Dad, I was just waving to Summer and Roman, who I met yesterday. Hopefully we can meet up again after I get back from Miami Beach."

"Sure, perhaps Axel here would like to join you? What, do you say Axel?"

Axel nodded, turning to his father who smiled and nodded, "That sounds like a good idea, Arthur. It will be some company for him, thank you."

"Come Daniel, we need to go, you can catch up with your friends later."

My father stood up, kissed my mothers' cheek and steered me by the shoulder away from the table and out of the dining room. The taxi took a slow drive across town to the coastline, eventually pulling up outside the Hotel Miami Beach. This was a much more modern building than the one we were staying in.

The entrance had a concierge at the door who wore red livery (in other words a porter, wearing very smart red trousers and jacket).

We walked into a large hall with modern paintings hanging on the walls. There was a central reception desk and a smartly dressed man behind it, "Can I help you sir?"

"Yes, we are looking for the elderly gentleman that was brought here last night from the Miami Hotel. He is expecting us."

"I'm sorry sir, do you know his name?"

"No, I'm afraid not, but he was very elderly, with a long beard."

"I'm sorry sir, but we have no guests who fit that description. You must have the wrong hotel."

"He must be here! He was brought here by the taxi we put him in it ourselves and gave the taxi driver the address. Our hotel receptionist rang here and told you to expect him plus he needed his room straight away. He must be here!"

"You're the one that must be mistaken sir."

"Daniel, there must be a simple explanation, perhaps the gentleman here was not working last night, therefore did not see him."

"With respect sir, I am not mistaken. We have no elderly guests; I can assure you. I was on duty all afternoon and evening yesterday; no new guests were checked in."

"Come on Dad, it's no use, if he is here then this man doesn't know him, if he isn't then we're just wasting time arguing. Maybe he changed his mind and got out of the taxi before it got here. He's clearly not here so we might as well go."

"I don't know Daniel, what if this man is wrong, and he is here somewhere. It seems strange that he hasn't booked in after all the fuss he made at our hotel. We shall go and get a drink in the coffee lounge and see if he turns up, I'm parched and could do with something to quench my thirst, before we tackle that heat outside. I'll ask the desk guy to order us a taxi and to let us know when it arrives."

I guessed Dad was stressed from the way he had spoken to the desk clerk, so I just nodded and followed him to the coffee lounge.

The minutes ticked by, our drinks came, various guests wandered in and out, some stopping for coffee others just meeting a friend and going off with them. By the time our taxi arrived, I felt we must have seen all the guests in the hotel except the one we were here to see.

"Come Daniel, this is pointless. We will have to make enquires with the cab firm from last night if you still wish to see him. He knows where you are staying so he can come and find you if he is desperate to see you. Let's go. Your mother will be wondering where we are, it's nearly lunch time."

Without a backward glance he strode out of the lounge toward the door, with myself a few steps behind, trying to keep up.

4: DANIEL'S RETURN

Told by Axel

He said it would all end in disaster, but we didn't listen, perhaps we should have but at the time it seemed like a good idea. I suppose I could have been more supportive at the time and not sided with the others, but they were pretty insistent, especially the girl. It's not really my fault, after all I hadn't met them before, and when Daniel introduced them to me it seemed like we had been friends a long time, I didn't understand why then, but it's different now.

Sorry, where are my manners, I should have introduced myself to you. My name is Axel, and I'm a new friend of Daniel's, he may have mentioned me to you, or maybe not.

I'm thirteen, and this is my first holiday in America. Come to that it's my first holiday anywhere. I tell everyone I'm an only child, but I'm not really, I have an older sister. She's ten years older than me, her names Portia, and she's sort of grown up, we don't play together like kids do.

My parents had her when they were young, or me when they were old, depending on your point of view.

We don't even look like brother and sister. She's got very blond hair that's all soft and curly, whereas mine's thick, dark brown and short. We get along most of the time, but we don't see much of each other as she's at work when I come home from school. I go to bed soon after she gets in.

Any way she hasn't come on holiday with us, so that's enough about her, and I'll continue. Where was I, oh yeah, Daniel.

Well, we had agreed to meet, after he had been to see some old man, so I was surprised to meet him coming through the front entrance on my way down from my room.

Anyway, let's not get ahead of ourselves, and I'll put you in the picture.

I was coming down the stairs into the foyer when Daniel and his Dad arrived back from their visit to see the old man. I didn't know who the man was, but I could see things had gone badly as they both looked glum.

"Hi Daniel, is it hot out there, have you had a good morning?" I said shyly, trying to ignore their glum faces. "

"He wasn't there."

"What you mean he had gone out, without waiting for you?"

"No, I mean he wasn't there at all, he hadn't booked in."

Then his Dad interrupted us." "Right, I'm off to find your mother, I'll meet with you later, don't forget lunch is at 1pm. Don't be late. Axel's parents will probably be expecting him there too."

We watched his Dad stroll over to the lift, like a man who had just shrugged off all responsibility for the days' events.

"I say, Daniel, did I say something wrong?"

"No, Dad's just cross because he's wasted the morning, taking me to see the man."

"It is jolly strange that he wasn't there."

"Oh well, no matter, Dad's not cross with you, he's just cross. Let's go and find the others and I'll introduce you to them. Ok follow me, we can start at the desk to see if they're in their rooms."

After we had separated at breakfast time, I had spent some time exploring the hotel, so I was keen to show Daniel around.

In our excitement we ran over to the reception desk clerk, "Are the children, Summer and Roman in their rooms?"

"No, young man, their keys are gone, they may have gone out."

"Oh bother!" Daniel responded, and turned on his heel, to walk away.

"Don't worry Daniel, I can be showing you the places they may be in the hotel, if we don't find them, they're bound to turn up for lunch."

"Oh alright, thanks Axel, lead on."

Without waiting for him to change his mind, I grabbed his arm, "Come on then, it's this way" and pulled him toward a side door.

I showed him the sports arena first. "Look Daniel, there's the swimming pool, and here's the changing rooms, oh, and there's a Sauna over here with shower rooms and lockers for your stuff. Outside those dark glass doors is an open lido, for when it's hot and sunny like today."

"Wow, they've thought of everything, let's see if the others are in there."

We pulled the doors apart and went into a bright, blinding light and intense heat. There was no sheltered area here, no air conditioning either, we were outside the hotel, in the garden area, where Palm trees provided a natural barrier, a slight relief from the hot rays of the sun, as their branches moved in response to a light breeze. To assist the comfort of the guests, a number of tables, with large umbrellas, were set round the pool perimeter. A bar with alcohol and soft drinks in one corner, and an ice cream stand in another. We searched the area, but couldn't find the others "Let's try the sports complex, maybe they are there." I led the way. There was a bowling green, a pitch and putt, mini golf green, tennis courts and bowling alley, all available to the guests, but no Roman or Summer.

We went into the other areas, where we found a library room, a card room, a coffee bar and lounge, and eventually the dining room.

I was doing my best to keep Daniel upbeat, but I could tell he was disappointed. We entered the dining room. The tables were all set, but no guests were present. A waiter was putting the finishing touches to the buffet table, checking that everything was in order. Daniel spun on his heel and walked out again.

"Let's go and get ready for lunch. We'll have to wait and see if they join us then. It's nearly 1 pm, my father will be expecting me to be clean and tidy, so I will need to go and change. It's a bit of a bind but you probably need to as well. We can meet back here in ten minutes. Ok?"

"Yes, that's swell, all that searching in the heat has made me feel a bit sweaty. I'll go and freshen up, meet you back here."

We separated and made for our hotel rooms. Daniel took the lift, whilst I went up the stairs. The morning hadn't been very fruitful, Daniel was still preoccupied with finding the others and about not having found the old man. He seemed partly annoyed that he had wasted time visiting the man, but also worried about him not being there as arranged.

He was also anxious to see Summer and Roman, to ask them if they had seen the old man whilst out on their travels that morning.

I hurried back to my room and found my parents waiting for me.

"Where have you been, you're late, you should have been back half an hour ago; never mind, you don't have time for explanations. Go and get yourself changed, be quick about it. I don't want to keep the whole lunch service waiting."

"Sorry Dad, I'll be quick."

I dashed into the bathroom for a quick wash, then the bedroom to change into long trousers and clean shirt.

"I'm ready, shall we go?"

Within a flash, we were out of the room and in the hallway. My parents chose to go in the lift, but I headed down the stairs. We reached the bottom at the same time to walk into the dining room together. It was crowded, I looked round to see if I could recognise anybody.

Daniel was at the table with his parents, but there was no sign of Summer or Roman. They must have opted for a packed lunch or just gone out to a restaurant. Little did I know at the time, that they were caught up in a difficult situation. What I did know, however, was that Daniel was going to be very disappointed if they didn't turn up soon.

Lunch passed uneventful, we were served with a choice of fish, meat, vegetables or rice, salad, fruit, coffee. Our parents chatted about the day's events. Daniel's father expressed his irritation and concern about the elderly man. My father acknowledged this and sought to reassure him that he had done all he could. Daniel's mother shrugged it off as the man being confused, as the rest of us just sat quietly, eating and listening.

It was as we were just finishing our meals, that the door to room was flung open and Roman and Summer came bounding in. They rushed over to our table, ignoring the waiter and their parents' calls to stop. "Quick, Daniel, you must come, we need to get the boat to the islands, our parents know why. They can talk to yours, to explain. Hurry there's no time, it goes in fifteen minutes from the quay."

Daniel looked at Summer and Roman, then turned to his parents.

"Ok Daniel, but don't be late back, is Axel going with you?"

Daniel turned to me and smiled, I returned his smile, he confirmed with our parents, and introduced me to Roman and Summer.

"Come on then both of you, we must hurry!" gasped Summer, with that we were dragged away from our table and out of the room.

"Hurry, I'll explain on the boat, Roman can fill in the details, can't you Roman?"

"Yes" and he waved a newspaper in the air and smiled.

5: A DAY TRIP TO BIG BAHAMA ISLAND

We arrived at the quay, just as the skipper was untying the ropes. "Wait, for us!" called Summer, "We're coming too!"

Jumping aboard, we thanked the skipper, and quickly found seats near the front.

Listening to the sound of the splashing waves and the engine and feeling the swell of the tide under the boat, I began to feel a bit queasy. I tried to focus on the conversation to make the feeling go away but I was conscious of my lunch stirring around in my tummy. I was not used to boats and I felt too embarrassed to say anything. I hoped that if I concentrated on the conversation, the feelings and nausea would pass.

So, I sat quietly and listened to Summer and Roman tell us about their morning, as well as their plan.

"We're sorry to drag you away like that, we had our lunch at the burger bar, and that's why we were late back."

"At least that's one reason."

"We had been out for the morning together. Our parents had booked a coach trip, arranged by the hotel. We went to some old fort that had been discarded a hundred years ago. We hadn't been there long, when some guys turned up, planning to stash their stuff there! Didn't they Summer?"

"Yes, they had loads of boxes and caused a bit of a commotion. You tell them, Roman."

"They were threatening to let the tyres down on the coach, if we didn't get out of there soon, so the driver gathered us all together again and got us onto the coach."

"We were then driven back to Miami and taken to a burger bar for lunch as compensation."

"That's all very well, Summer, but what's all that got to do with dragging us across town to catch this boat?"

"Hey, Roman, can you show Daniel the newspaper article? Oh, his friend may want to see it too?"

"Ok, look guys, this is why you're here!"

He opened the newspaper and pointed to a boxed advert that had been highlighted.

HELP REQUIRED TO SOLVE THE MYSTERY OF THE MISSING MAN AND HIS STAFF.

An elderly gentleman was reported missing after he had reported that his staff had been stolen at the Miami airport.

The gentleman was due to attend a special convention, regarding precious artefacts, but did not arrive at his hotel.

It is known that he initially tried to book into the wrong hotel but was subsequently put in a taxi, which was hired by the hotel staff to take him to his correct destination.

It is now known that he did not arrive and his whereabouts and that of the taxi are unknown.

There is concern for the Professor's welfare due to his frail health and poor knowledge of the Miami area.

It is possible that the taxi driver had misunderstood the instructions and taken him to one of the islands by mistake.

If anyone has any knowledge of his whereabouts or that of the taxi driver, then please can they report to the Miami Detective Agency.

A substantial reward will be paid for his safe return and that of his staff.

"I don't understand. Daniel, and I know that or at least most of it. You tell them Daniel, after all it's your story from this morning, not mine."

Daniel:

"Okay, well after we left the airport last night and went to book in at the hotel, we were surprised to see the elderly gentleman having a row with the reception person. She was all flustered, trying to make him understand that his name wasn't on the list of reservations. Anyhow when he showed her his ticket it became apparent that he had made a mistake and needed the Miami Beach hotel. Well, he collapsed again like he did at the airport, so my Mum stepped in and gave the receptionist orders. One of which was to call him a cab and send him to the correct hotel. My Dad and I helped him get into the cab with his luggage, and the driver was given the details of where to go. The old man had asked me to promise that I would visit him the following morning, which was today. So, I and my, Dad confirmed it. After breakfast Dad and I went over to the hotel, only to find that he hadn't been there and hadn't booked in. Dad and I hung around for a while in case he turned up, then returned to our own hotel. When we returned, Axel and I looked round our hotel, but there was no sign of him."

"Summer, I still don't understand why we have had to come on this boat!"

"Don't you see, I thought it was obvious. The old guy needs our help, we need to find him and his staff."

"That's all very well, Summer, but we don't have any clues and we don't even know if his staff is an object or a team of people!"

"Oh, but we do, at least we think we might have a clue. In the advert it says that the old man was put in a taxi, that didn't arrive. Well, you see, Roman and I saw an old man this morning remonstrating with a taxi driver, (for those of you who don't know what, remonstrating means, well it's an adult word for arguing). They eventually drove off toward the quay. We didn't see the old guy's face, but I'm sure it was him."

"What about you Roman, do you think the same?"

"The truth is I'm not so sure it was him but agree we should check it out."

"Well, I'm still not sure that this is a good idea; there are lots of old men in taxis, most of whom may argue with their driver. We could just be on a wild goose chase and end up looking silly or even worse, we could all end up in trouble!"

"Oh, don't be such a pain, Daniel, it could be fun, we have never been to the islands, and I for one would like to explore it. Let's face it, we are on holiday after all, what say you two?"

"I agree with Summer, what about you Axel, are you in too?"

"Well, Daniel is right, we don't know if it's him or how it will turn out, but it would be an adventure. What do you reckon Daniel? After all, it's best if we stick together and you did promise to help the old man."

"Oh ok, you're right, we are on holiday, and it would be fun to have a quest and explore the islands, but don't say I didn't warn you if we end up in trouble or danger."

"Hooray! We're going on an adventure, all four of us together, thanks boys, I knew we could have fun together when I met you all."

"That's enough now Summer, we all agree, but we need to plan how we are going to find the old man and his staff."

"You're right Roman, but first of all we need a name for our quest, what say you, Daniel?"

"Sure, I think we should call it the Quest for the Stolen Staff. What do you think Axel?"

"Well, it's a start, we can always change it later, when we get there."

"I know, instead of the Quest for the Stolen Staff, why don't we call it the Mystery Four and the Quest for the Stolen Staff? After all, that is what we are isn't it?"

"Why Roman, that's brilliant? Don't you agree Daniel and Summer?"

"Why yes, I like that."

"Me too"

"And me."

"Well boys that's settled, we're the mystery four, on the quest for the missing man and his stolen staff."

"Shhh Summer, not too loud, we don't want anyone overhearing us. We must be careful, there may be spies on board, you know other people looking for it too. Or even those that stole it in the first place!"

"Sorry Daniel, it was the excitement, you're right, we have to be careful. Let's find a spot where we can't be overheard."

We picked up the newspaper, and then looked around for a quiet spot on the boat. "Over there, everyone, there's no one up the back, everyone is up front watching the distance disappear between us and the island."

Axel, Summer and Roman turned to see where I was pointing, sure enough the rear of the boat was empty as far as they could see. We found a seat and huddled together in conversation.

"Summer, try and keep your voice down, or I fear we will be overheard."

"Sorry Daniel, I forgot, I'll try and whisper."

In our haste to hatch out a plan, we forgot to keep watch, and were therefore not aware, at the time, if we were being overheard. Without getting too far ahead in my story, this later proved to be disastrous, causing much difficulty and mayhem.

After about ten minutes, we had decided that we would contact the person who put the advert in the paper to find out more about the old man. We needed to know why someone would wish to kidnap him, also what his staff was, and why someone would want to steal it or them.

We were not sure if the paper would give us any details as we were children. I suggested, however, that maybe I could make enquires as he had asked me to visit him, which I had done with my Dad. This may persuade them that even though I was only a child, I should be given some explanation, in exchange for what I could tell them.

It was agreed therefore that I would go to the newspaper office on Big Bahama Island and seek the name of the person placing the advert. Axel would go with me, to keep an eye out for any people following us.

Roman and Summer were going to visit some of the boarding houses and hotels, to enquire if the old man, or should I say Professor, had checked into any of them since he went missing.

We would meet up again in two hours at the quay and update each other.

6: THE START OF OUR QUEST ADVENTURE

The Children pair off:

Daniel & Axel set off from the quay together

When the boat docked, we made our way to the gang plank, that enabled us to leave the boat and step onto the jetty.

Axel and I went ahead of the other two as the boat was crowded, people were pushing and shoving in their eagerness to disembark. Poor old Axel was feeling somewhat queasy. He had tried to hide it, but I could tell by the green tinge he had over his face and his constant gasping. He staggered a bit down the gangplank, his legs buckling under him. I grabbed him, saying "Come on old boy, let's explore the island," and steered him onto the jetty and off toward the bars and shops that lined the quayside.

I turned to look back just as Roman and Summer climbed off the boat onto the jetty. As I did so, I had a strange feeling that danger was lurking round them.

There was a swarthy young man, of about 25 years of age, a few inches behind them. He did not appear to be carrying anything and he looked as if he was used to boats, for he was nimble of foot when on the gangplank. He showed no difficulty in stepping ashore.

He looked like a tourist or visitor to the island, yet he gave me a cold feeling, the sense of danger came over me the closer he got to them.

As I turned away again, I heard a scream, and a loud scraping noise. I turned around and there was Summer, lying flat on her face, her feet and arms stretched out trying to grab the metal sides of the jetty. I was about to run back and help her when Axel stopped me saying, "No Daniel, don't go back. It's not safe. Let Roman help her, he will know what to do. If you go back, you may put us all in danger as they will be seeking to trap us in some way."

"We can't just leave her" I said, as I tried to turn toward her. Grabbing my arm to stop me he said, "Yes, we can. We must. You felt the danger as I did, and you saw the young guy behind her. I'm not sure of his game, but I know he is planning something to either help or hinder us finding the old man or completing the quest."

I sensed he was right, so we stood watching from a distance, whilst the young man behind her helped her up, and introduced himself. It was all over within a few minutes. Both Roman and Summer appeared to be okay and able to continue their journey unhindered. I, however, could not shake off the feeling of distrust and danger that I felt when the young man was present. Axel appeared disturbed by him also, and we decided to keep an eye out for him when we were seeking to find the old man.

Putting it to the back of our minds, we hurried on to find the newspaper office. Fortunately for us, most of the people in the

Bahama's, which was the name of the island we had come to, spoke an Americanised form of English. We could therefore ask them for direction and be understood. It wasn't long before someone pointed us in the direction of a large newspaper print works. It was a sprawling stone building at the end of a long parade of buildings, all shapes and sizes.

Axel was still feeling a bit washed out from the boat trip, so we refreshed ourselves at a kiosk selling skewers of spiced meat and coke, before going into the building.

As we entered the front of the building, we could hear the sound of people typing and shuffling papers. The sound of printing presses clattered in the background and a smell of print ink hung in the air.

We had entered into a world of fast-moving information; people were running about trying to get their stories to the print room in time for the deadline.

We went unnoticed for some few minutes before someone accidentally bumped into us and dropped all their newspaper clippings at our feet. Annoyed at our presence, he laid into us.

"What are you doing in here? Who let you in? How dare you get in my way! Can't you see we're all busy? Get out, you're not welcome!"

Overhearing his tirade toward us, a young lady who was dressed very smartly, walked over and interrupted him. "That's enough Jack, you'll frighten the lads, why don't we see what they want before you eat them for breakfast?"

She looked down at us, as we were trying to pick up the spilt paper clippings. "Thanks boys, but you can leave that now."

Jack glared at us as we stood up, "Answer me and Jane then, what are you doing here?"

Backing away slightly, I turned toward the lady that I now knew to be called Jane.

"We are really sorry to have caused a problem, we came here to find out the name of the person who put the advert in the paper about the reward for information about the missing Professor"

"You see he asked me to visit him and when Dad and I went to see him at the hotel, he wasn't there. We wanted to help find him, because he seemed a nice old man."

"It's more like you want the reward, get lost."

"No honest we don't, we want to help him."

"I don't believe you, get out."

"No wait Jack let's hear them out, they could be legit."

I noticed Axel had wandered off toward the printing presses, so I quickly distracted them saying at a rapid pace, "I met the old man at the airport. He was complaining of his staff being stolen. He wasn't making a lot of sense as he didn't seem to have any one with him, so we thought he must be lost whilst his staff were looking for him. He argued with the security guard and fainted." I stopped, mid-sentence, as they were both laughing.

"I don't understand, what's so funny?"

"You are boy, he wasn't looking for people, he was looking for a staff, you know, like a shepherd crook, a walking stick, they use for herding the sheep. You know like Merlin had in King Arthur."

I stepped back, feeling a complete fool. Of course, he was right, we had completely misunderstood. Gathering my wits, I replied meekly, "Surely no-one would want to steal a tall walking stick?"

"Oh, but lad, this is no ordinary walking stick. This is a historic artefact of a precious metal and of great value."

"Oh! I'm sorry I didn't know."

Jane quickly came to my rescue. "You weren't to know, Jack stop teasing him, and let the boy continue with his information. So far, he is the only one who has come forward with any information and shown any concern about the old guy."

"Carry on kid, what happened to the old guy at the airport?"

"Well, he kept saying his staff had been stolen, then he passed out and the security guy took him to an interview room. He asked us to go with him and explain what was upsetting the man. Then after my Mum finished telling him what had happened, we were dismissed. As no longer needed, we went to our hotel. When we got there, he was arguing with the receptionist, saying that he was booked in. The receptionist said he wasn't, and that he couldn't have a room as they were fully booked. He fainted again. The receptionist asked to see his reservation and found that he was at the wrong hotel.

My Mum told the reception lady to call a taxi to take him to the Miami Beach hotel. When it arrived, we put him and his luggage in it and told the taxi driver where to go. He kept asking me for help and insisted I promise to visit him today. So, my Dad agreed we could, but when we went there, we found he hadn't booked in. So, we left. Then my friends showed me the article in the paper, so I came here to find out if you knew who put it in. To help us find him."

"Well, I'm sorry lad, but we are not allowed to divulge our source's identity. I suggest you see if the advert gives you any other information that can lead you to him."

"Come on Jane, we have wasted enough time on this kid and his friend. There is nothing we can do for them. Can you show them out please?"

"Okay, Jack. Sorry, but you will have to leave now." Turning toward Axel she called, "That goes for you too."

"Wait, can't we even talk to the guy who wrote the article, after all the advert does mention a reward for help to find him, or his staff?"

"Sure you can, but you will have to come back next month, he's on a vacation, out of the country."

"He must have left some information we can use, after all the advert didn't say he wasn't available."

"Sure he did, and I just told you he's out of the country, so to come back next month. You got it, he ain't available. Jane, will you get these kids out of here before I have them arrested for trespassing."

"Sure, come on kids, you heard him, out you go."

I called Axel who was standing a few feet away, looking

through the doorway into a print office. He turned immediately and joined me, politely turning to the lady called Jane, to thank her for her help.

It didn't register at the time, but I later realised that he hadn't been present for any of the conversation that I had with Jane and Jack.

We left the building and walked back the way we had come. Axel appeared preoccupied with his own thoughts, so I didn't interrupt them.

As we passed the coffee stand from before, I realised that we had been in the building for a good hour or more. This, added to our journey time, amounted to more than a couple of hours since we had left the others. We needed to quicken our pace if we were to get back to the boat in time for its return sailing.

"Axel, hurry please or we will miss the boat"

The urgency in my voice registered and he started to run. When we arrived back at the boat, there was no sign of the other two. We scoured the quayside from the boat deck, but neither Roman nor Summer were there.

The boat was due to leave soon, we persuaded the skipper to hang on a bit longer, but it soon became apparent that they would not return in time.

As the boat pulled away, I recalled the incident on the key earlier that day. I recalled the closeness of the young man behind Summer and the sense of danger returned, making me shiver.

7: THINGS GO FROM BAD TO WORSE

Roman & Summer set off from the quay together.

Told by Roman

After Axel and Daniel left us, Summer and I descended the jetty to make our way to the quayside. Or at least that's what we attempted to do. I was unaware that we were being followed at the time. So, I was surprised when Summer suddenly came crashing forward, landing flat on her face.

As she scrabbled at the sides of the jetty with her hands, I felt a hand in the middle of my back, "Out of the way boy," the voice commanded. I was pushed aside by a swarthy young man in his mid-twenties. As I staggered, trying to regain my balance, he bent down and within a flash lifted Summer to her feet.

Gasping for air and tears rolling down her face, she eyed him with suspicion, then meekly said "Thank you." It was a strange look she initially gave him, but soon changed her expression to a smile.

Looking at me she indicated for me to do the same, acknowledging her look I turned to the guy. "Why, yes sir, thank you for helping my friend. We are in your debt."

"Nonsense boy, I could see the young girl had fallen, glad I could help."

“Well thank you again.” I took hold of Summer’s arm.

“Come on Summer, we must hurry, people are waiting to get off the jetty.”

With that I gave her a tug. I felt a strange atmosphere and an urgency to be gone. “Let's find a first aid place on the quay and get those scratches and bruises attended to.”

Sensing the urgency, in my voice and feeling embarrassed, Summer agreed, soon we were quickly leaving the jetty and moving along the quayside.

As we got out of earshot she stopped. Turning toward me blurted out, “He pushed me, I know he did!”

“Who?” I said not needing to be told, as I had felt a strangeness in her initial look and the atmosphere.

“That man silly, who else? He pushed me then pretended to help me, I know he did.”

“We need to be very careful; it seems that someone is out to get us or stop us finding the old man.”

“I don't understand, why? He came after me and pushed me over, then picked me up. It doesn't make sense, we didn't tell anyone where we were going or what we were doing.”

“I agree, he must have been following us, or overheard what we said when with the others.”

“It seems strange that he has just let us carry on walking away and not stopped us or come after us.”

“Maybe he has another plan, we need to be extra vigilant, but if we see him again, we must pretend we don't suspect him. Agreed?”

"Yes agreed."

Having confirmed our decision, we carried on walking. It wasn't long before we bumped into him again. This time it was in a bar. We had stopped to get Summer a bottle of water, to help bathe her knee. The graze on her right knee was giving her pain and bleeding.

We hadn't been in there long before the guy came in.

"Hey, you ok? You went off so quick, I thought I must have upset you?"

"We're fine, thanks, just wanted to get some water to get cleaned up." I said, pointing to Summer's knee.

"Well now, do you fancy a coke each? I'm buying, after all you've had a bit of a shock, the sugar in it will do you good."

"Okay thanks," called Summer, who was bent over her knee, "that's very kind of you."

"Yes thanks, we would like to accept, Summer will be ready in a minute, shall we sit over there?" I said pointing, as I walked over to a table near the door, which I chose in case Summer, and I needed a quick getaway.

He bought the coke and came and joined me. Summer, took a few more minutes, then, sat down with us.

"Cheers!" I raised my can, and they followed suit, we all drank from them.

"Are you following us?"

"No, I saw you through the window, and thought I'd check

you were okay, that's all. How's your drinks?"

"Fine thanks, we are grateful, what's your name?"

"It's Jethro, what's yours?"

"Mine is Summer, this is my friend Roman."

"Why you here on Big Bahama Island?"

"We're on holiday, and just visiting to have a look around, we thought we would get a boat to the islands to see what was here."

"Is that all, nothing else?"

"No, just exploring for a couple of hours, away from our parents. they know we have come but said we could come without them, as it's our holiday adventure."

We finished our drinks then left the bar, to continue our journey.

"Would you like me to show you round? After all, I have lived here a long time, I know all the tourist spots."

"Don't you have any work to do or somewhere else to be?" I asked.

"No not today, it's my holiday too, I have the whole week off. I am at your service."

"Thanks for the offer, but we can manage. We don't want to take up your holiday time."

"Oh, but I insist. You will be good company, I hadn't any plans."

I sensed a sound of menace in his voice, and turned to look at Summer, I could see that her eyes were wide with fear, but she quickly shook it off.

"Come on Roman, let's see the sights with Jethro. We can spend an hour with him, before we have to get back to the boat."

Summer was clearly giving me a sign, to not upset him and play along with him.

"That's settled then, come on both of you, there's no time to waste. If we keep on this road we will come to the centre where there are lots of places to see."

We carried on walking. As we did so, I noticed a number of boards advertising snorkelling, fishing and golfing, in addition to boards advertising trips round the islands.

I found out much later that we had come to the largest of the islands. That there was approximately seven hundred of them in total, of varying shape, size and habitation.

The one we were on was surrounded by a deep blue sea, that lapped at beautiful beaches of white sand. There were rich, bright coloured flowers with strong aroma, lavish green vegetation, and scenery.

We passed houses and bars, and people sitting on the roadside, selling their wares, before eventually reaching the centre, or marketplace as it clearly was.

The hustle and bustle of people was a contrast to the road we had come along. Although the quayside had been busy, most of the people had dissipated quite quickly whilst we had been tending to Summer's injuries. We had passed some on the road, but none as many as we found in the market square.

Music was mingled with the sound of voices, people selling their goods, buyers haggling over prices. There were animals, bars and cafes, around the perimeter, with the smell of meat and fish, rich coffee and spices filling the air. It was a heady atmosphere, and Summer and I soon forgot our concerns about Jethro, as he directed us through crowds and stalls, whilst enabling us to see all that was on show.

We became so engrossed in what we were looking at, that it was some time before I realised that we were running late for getting back to the boat. I turned to tell Summer this and noticed she was no longer beside me, neither was Jethro. I didn't think too much of it at first, thinking that they had probably gone to the next stall or ducked inside one to have a look at something at the back of one. I wandered on to the next few stalls, expecting to find them, but there was no sign of them, I called them, struggling to make my voice heard over the noise of music and chatter, but received no response in reply.

I increased my speed and efforts to find them, constantly checking my watch, worried that we would miss the boat back to the mainland. I did not relish the thought of being stranded here. I didn't think Summer would be too keen either. I had spent a good half hour searching for them to no avail, before thinking that I was an idiot and they had probably made their way back to the boat, not realising that I wasn't following them. I called them loudly once more, I listened, using my extra sensitive hearing but heard nothing from them, so I turned and with my best speed, made my way back toward the quayside to try and catch them up at the boat.

I hadn't realised how far we had come. I knew that the ferry took about two hours or more to get here and would take about the same to get back. I guessed we would be allowed four or five hours on the island itself. This knowledge calmed me a little for although we had been here a number of hours, I was sure it had not been as long as four.

I would at least have time to meet up with the others, even if I couldn't find Summer. They would surely help.

I stopped a few times along the way to ask travellers if they had seen Summer or Jethro. "No, sorry young man, no one like that has gone through here." I then asked them if they had seen Daniel or Axel? "No sir, you should try the beach, or the caves, or maybe they've stumbled into the jungle and been eaten by wild beasts!"

The sound of their laughter rang in my ears as I carried on my search.

The sun was dropping down and the air was cooler, night time wasn't far off. I quickened my pace. Suddenly there was a shriek, I realised it was my own voice as I fell face forward to the ground. I had been pounced on, but as I struggled, all I could hear was laughter. My arms were grabbed as I was pulled to my feet.

"Hold still, we've got you!"

I turned to find Jethro and Summer, laughing, as if they thought it funny to jump me.

"Where have you been? I have hunted everywhere for you," I

demanded angrily, smarting from their silly prank.

"Calm down! We were busy exploring and lost sight of you, so we thought you must have gone back to the ferry. We were right, weren't we?"

"Yes, but only because I was worried about Summer, and came back to find her."

"I was so worried; I haven't had a chance to look for anyone else."

"What do you mean, who else were you looking for?"

I gulped, "Er, well no one!"

"He means Axel and Daniel, our friends, Jethro. Don't you Roman?"

"Yes, of course I do, who else is there?"

"Come on then, let's get back to the ferry, and see if they are there. Do you mind if I lean on you a bit Jethro, my leg is still a bit sore?" "Okay, come on then."

With that we walked back to the ferry boat quay. I realised I had nearly given the game away, but Summer had stepped in, just in time.

8: THE FERRY LEAVES WITHOUT US: WHAT NOW?

Told by Daniel:

I was startled out of my thoughts by the sound of the ferry boat engine, as it pulled out of the harbour.

"What happens now? They could be anywhere on the island."

"I agree, Axel, maybe they are just late."

"Let's hope so."

"Let's hope they haven't come to any harm, I didn't like the way Summer fell on the jetty, I'm sure she was pushed."

"We need to be careful Daniel, there are people out there who may try and prevent us finding the professor."

"Yes, you're right, and I for one don't trust that guy who picked her up when she fell."

"Shush Daniel, look they're coming and he's with them."

"Hi, you're late, the ferry boat has gone. What kept you?"

"It's gone, oh no, you're kidding, it can't have! We've got to get home tonight!"

"What kept you? Axel and I tried to get them to delay, which they did for a while, but they couldn't wait any longer."

"Why didn't you go with them?"

"I should have thought that was obvious, we were worried about Summer and Roman, we didn't want to leave them stranded."

"By the way, who are you?"

"Oh sorry, this is Jethro. I fell on the jetty when we were getting off, and he helped me to my feet again. He has shown us round the island. We're sorry we are late, we got separated from Roman and time went by without us realising. It was quite late by the time we managed to meet up again."

"Jethro, this is Daniel and Axel, our friends from the hotel."

"Well, we're all here now. So, we need to find a boat to take us back to the mainland."

"What if there aren't any more tonight?"

"If there aren't any Summer, we will have to find a hotel for the night!"

"Oh no Mum and Dad, won't be happy about that!"

"Probably not Summer! Let's not get ahead of ourselves."

"Why don't we go and explore the ferry services, there must be more than one boat that goes between here and the mainland."

"My thoughts exactly Axel, come on guys, this way."

"Thanks Jethro, for your kindness to Summer and Roman, maybe we'll see you again sometime."

"Yes, thanks Jethro, it was kind of you to show Roman and me round the island. I hope you have a good week off over here."

"Come on guys we had better hurry, if we're going to find another boat sailing tonight."

"Bye Jethro."

We left Jethro standing there, surprised that we had dismissed him. I couldn't help thinking that he was a danger to us all, and our mission. Yet, I had nothing concrete to go on. I picked up vibes that the others didn't trust him but were doing their best not to show it.

As I said, I knew this would lead us into trouble, and I was right.

Had I known then what I know now, I would have been pleased that we were stranded on the island. Perhaps I should explain.

9: BACK AT HOTEL MIAMI THE PARENTS MEET

Unknown to us at the time, our parents were spending time together, back on the mainland.

They had continued with their meal, after the disruption from Summer and Roman, fully aware that when we all left together for a boat trip to the islands, that we would probably have fun and enjoy our freedom, and possibly miss the first boat back.

So, with those thoughts in mind, they relaxed into what they thought would be an afternoon of freedom and enjoyment for themselves.

Well, why don't I let them explain, as if I was a fly on the wall, watching and listening in to their conversation.

You will see what I mean, here goes:

"Well, we won't see those four for a few hours, so we may as well finish our meal here and go grab a drink in the bar, what say you, Tobias?"

"A splendid idea Arthur, what do you say ladies, shall we adjourn to the bar?"

Jean and Annalisa looked at each other, sighed then smiled toward the men and replied in unison, "We would love too!"

"Well, if we are all finished let's go. Lead the way Toby, Jean and I will follow you."

They entered the bar, the smell of fresh ground coffee hung in the air, mixed with the smell of alcohol. The room was set with small tables, and a number, of residents were already present, having adjourned from the dining room to partake of coffee and liqueurs.

They were shown to a table, but as they were about to sit down, Arthur noticed a couple who he thought were Summer's parents, sitting at a table in the corner of the room.

"Look folks, if I'm not mistaken that's Summer's parents over there. What do you think Jean? Are they?"

"Well Arthur, I must say they look like the couple from the airport that were with Summer. Why don't you go and ask them? You can invite them to join us for a coffee or drink."

"Ok love, you go and sit down, with the others, I won't be long."

Arthur approached the couple, introduced himself, and confirmed that they were Summer's parents.

"Would you care to join us? My wife and I have a table just over there with Axel's parents. I believe the children have all joined forces, possibly to hunt down the old guy, perhaps we can do the same?"

"I'm not sure what you mean, my husband and I would be

agreeable to joining you for a drink, I'm not sure about the rest of your suggestion."

"Well, to be honest, the idea just came to me, and I blurted it out without thinking, I'm sorry if I worried you."

"Please come and join us, and maybe we can discuss it further. By the way my name is Arthur, I'm Daniel's father. My wife's name is Jean. Axel's parents are Annalisa and Tobias, Toby for short."

"Ok, we will join you, my name is Rebecca and my husband here's called Jed. Summer went off with Roman saying that they were going to find Daniel, and I take it Axel was with him. We agreed that they could all go to the islands together, provided all the parents were in agreement. They are due to return on the ferry before the evening meal."

"Come."

They shook hands, then went across to the table where the others were waiting.

After further introductions, they all sat down, the waiter came and took their order and returned with their drinks. The women had coffee and the men, brandy.

"All we need now is Roman's parents to join us and then we will be complete."

"Well, you're in luck Arthur, they are just coming through the door."

Arthur and Jed stood up and walked toward them. As they did so, Jed signalled to Roman's parents to join us and as they came over, he explained to Arthur that they had met previously, when the children had met at the airport."

"Hi Jed, how's your day been? Is Rebecca not with you?"

"Yeah, she' over there at our table, we're all having coffee and liqueurs. We thought you may like to join us. By the way this is Arthur, he's Daniel's Dad, his wife and Axel's parents are with us. As all the kids went off together, we thought we would all have a drink together, sociable like."

"Sure, why not? Lead the way."

They all went over to the table, Jed introduced Roman's parents, Stefan and Selina to the others. They all shook hands and made room for them at the table.

Introductions were completed, then further drinks ordered from the bar.

"It's good to see the children are enjoying themselves and have made friends with each other, but I'm a bit worried that they may lead each other astray. Not intentionally, but in their attempt to have fun and explore the island."

"I'm inclined to agree with you Rebecca, after all they were a bit hyped up this morning about something, and in a hurry to catch the boat."

"I know, Roman said something about a newspaper article, didn't he Stefan?"

"Yes Selina, he said something about showing it to Daniel."

"That's funny they didn't mention it when they rushed into the dining room, saying about needing to catch the boat did they Jean?"

"No Annalisa, but I do recall Roman carrying one, which when you come to think of it, it was a bit odd, after all they don't usually read newspapers at their age do, they?"

"Is that why you made that remark about the professor, Arthur?"

"What comment was that, Arthur?"

"I'm sorry Jean, it was just a thought that I blurted out when I asked Rebecca and Jed to join us. I said the children had all joined forces to hunt for the old man, so we may as well do the same, to be sociable. I know Daniel was pretty upset about him going missing and I guess the other children were too."

"In that case we better get hold of a copy of that newspaper to see what bright idea they have got in their heads. What's do you reckon folks."

Jean looked at the others, one by one they nodded.

"Hold your horses a minute, maybe there's a quicker way, this is a hotel right, and they have newspapers delivered here daily, we can ask the waiter to fetch a copy of today's papers for us."

With that, Jed called the waiter and requested a set of the day's papers be brought to them, as well as a pot of coffee, fresh cups, and pen and paper. He gave the waiter his room number, to have it put on his bill.

Ten minutes later they were scouring the newspapers, over their coffee.

"This must be it!" everyone turned to look at Arthur. "There's an advert here requesting information about the whereabouts of a professor."

"Yes, but there's one beneath it, about exploring the islands for a true adventure. That's more likely. Look Arthur, it's in the 'Bahama times', that must be why they were so desperate to catch the boat to the island."

"Yes Jean, I think you're right."

"Well, what do we do now?"

Aware that there was a conflict of opinion, Arthur considered the question carefully before replying.

"As I see it, we have two options, we either sit tight and wait for them to come back for dinner and ask them about their day."

"And the other option Arthur?"

"We get the next boat over to the island and see if we can find them or the old professor guy."

"Well, I don't know about the rest of you, but I'm for staying here. I'm sure they will soon forget about any professor, once they have landed on the island. They will be far more interested in where they are than any old guy you call the professor."

"I agree"

"Me too"

"Count us in. Why go running after them, let them have their adventure, while we relax here."

"Okay, we will stay, then they can tell us all about their adventures when they return."

Clearly the other parents were more inclined to sit back and relax than chase after the children.

"Ok, let's do that, you're probably right."

They sat together for another half hour or so chatting, before they were interrupted by the waiter.

"Excuse me, sirs, but these gentlemen wish to speak with you."

"We're sorry to interrupt, but we need to speak to the person or persons who assisted an elderly gentleman into a cab last night."

"That was me, who are you? and why do you wish to know?"

"I am Lieutenant Green, from the Miami Police, and this is Detective Brown. Please can you come with us as we need to question you about the abduction of this elderly man."

"Well, I don't know anything about an abduction, all I did was put him in the taxi when it arrived and gave the driver the address of the hotel in Miami beach. The Miami hotel receptionist called the cab for him."

"Nevertheless sir, we would like you to come with us, according to our information you are the last person to have contact with him, and until he is found we are holding you responsible for his disappearance."

"But that's ridiculous, I had nothing to do with it, I tell you. Jean, tell him."

"That's true sir he just helped him into the cab."

"Either you come quietly sir, and help us with our enquires, or we will arrest you on the spot for obstructing police enquires and possible abduction."

"So much for a relaxing afternoon, I'm sorry folks, it looks like

I'm going to have to go with these guys."

"Jean, you stay here, I shouldn't be long, I haven't done anything wrong, I'll catch up with you later."

"Ok you two, I'll come with you, but I think you have it all wrong. I know nothing about this man's abduction."

"A wise decision sir. Come."

With that they left the bar, as the rest of the parents looked on in bewilderment.

10: DANIEL – MAROONED ON BIG BAHAMA ISLAND

Well, as you can imagine, when I found out what had happened to my father, I was concerned for his welfare but that is getting ahead of ourselves. I shall return now to our situation on the island.

Having missed the ferry boat and said goodbye to Jethro, we had made our way to the next bay to see if we could get a boat to the mainland.

We were faced with a dilemma, as the same situation occurred, we were too late. The last ferry had left. The only options open to us were to try and hire a boat or sail ourselves. We needed to find a boat owner and persuade them to take us across from the island to the mainland or find a bed and breakfast or hotel for the night.

It was getting dark, and we were beginning to realise that we were stranded on an island that we did not know.

"Let's count our money to see if we have enough cash between us to hire a boat, pay a ferry fare or for bed and breakfast somewhere."

"Well, I've got 10 dollars, Summer what you got?"

"I've got 15 dollars."

"I've got 12 dollars, so that makes 37 so far, Axel what about you?"

"Sorry I've only got 9 dollars 50 cents which only brings us to a total of 46 dollars 50 cents."

"That's not going to go far, can anyone remember how much ferry tickets cost. I don't think we are going to have enough."

With very little money between us we walked on to try and find a willing boatman to ferry us across the 70 miles to the mainland.

We had walked round to the next bay and were just giving up, when we came across a boatman who was willing to take us across to the mainland. We were delighted, however, he then told us he would not do so until the next morning.

"But we only have money for our boat journey!" I exclaimed.

"You can sleep in the boathouse for the night? Yer'll find a box in the back with blankets in it. The floor's hard but there's a couch the young lady can use."

"If it's food yer wanting, you'll have to catch a fish or two and build yerselves a fire down there on the beach. Unless yer changed yer mind. What say yer, do yer wanna seal the deal?"

"Sure" and we all shook hands.

The boathouse was small, most of the room was taken up by a small sailing boat. The mast of which was laid down, sails folded into the beam. Around the sides were lobster pots and nets, underwater snorkels and equipment. At the rear of the boat house was a day bed, with pillows and blankets, thrown in a heap on it. As the boatman had said there were more blankets in a box nearby.

"I suppose Summer should have the bed and the rest of us the floor, we can share the blankets and cushions amongst us. What do you say Summer, are you okay with that?"

"Well yes, but it seems so unfair on the rest of you."

"Well, it's just for one night, I'm sure we can manage. So why don't we go and catch some fish and cook it on the beach?"

"Okay, but you lot go ahead, I'll just sort out some space here for us all to sleep then join you. I won't be long."

"There's some matches over on that shelf in case you need them, I'm sure the guy won't mind us using a few, after all he suggested catching and cooking fish."

"Ok Summer, we'll get going."

The boys left the boat house and made their way down to the beach. Summer watched them until they had gone from view, so that she knew in what direction they went.

Turning back to the task in hand she moved a few baskets and pieces of equipment to clear an area close to the bed. She didn't fancy being there alone, so set the cushions and blankets out close by to enable them to be together.

She was just finishing, when she heard a footstep behind her. Just as she was about to turn around and enquire as to who it was, she was hit hard across the back of her head. The floor came up and hit her, and she lay there, motionless.

Her assailant checked the boat house to ensure no one else was hiding in it or nearby, then grabbing one of the blankets, wrapped it round summer and slung her over his shoulder, checking there was no one near the door, carried her out, and into the night.

Meanwhile the boys, were paddling around in the bay. Looking for fish. The water was clear and warm.

"There are loads of little fish over here, we can catch a few of these, I'm sure and they won't take long to cook."

"Axel, can you see if you can find some driftwood to make a fire with, and some that we can use to spear the fish, we will need quite a few as we don't have knives and forks. I wonder what we would have had back at the hotel."

"Probably a four-course meal, oh well not to worry, this is much more fun."

"Axel, lay the sticks for the fire over there and give the others to Roman to pierce the fish with."

"Now where did I put those matches? Oh! here they are."

Daniel pulled the box of matches from his back pocket; with a few quick movements he had set the wood into a kind of pile that was encased in a pyramid of sticks. Then he ripped a small piece off the bottom of his shirt to make a touch paper and lit it with a match. The flame grew slowly at first, then faster and higher, the twigs were dry and soon caught, giving off a crackling sound.

"Ok guys, it's ready to cook the fish on, not too many at a time though, or you will put it out."

They rested the fish on the outside of the pyramid, to bake, rather than be burnt straight away by the flames.

"Summer's taking a long time to join us, I wonder what's keeping her?"

"Don't worry Daniel, she's probably tried out the couch and fallen asleep."

"Your probably right Roman, I dare say we can always take her some back, she is bound to wake up as soon as we get back there."

"How much fish have we got?"

"I count fifteen, which if I'm not mistaken leaves us one short for four each."

"Well spotted Roman, perhaps we can draw lots to find out who gets one less than the rest of us?"

"What say you, Axel?"

"Well to be honest with you both, my tummy still feels a bit queasy, so I'll opt to only have three. The rest can be shared between you."

"That's mighty good of you Axel, sorry to hear your tummy still feels a bit squiffy."

"Thanks Daniel. I don't understand it, I haven't normally had this problem when sailing, I wonder if it is something I ate. If I didn't feel hungry, I would say to eat them all, and not have any myself. I am, however, starving as I haven't eaten for hours, so I will have a few as we don't know when or where the next meal will be available."

"We should all eat while it's hot, and then we can take some back to Summer. So, let's eat."

The boys helped themselves to the sticks and ate the hot fish that had been leaning against the fire pyramid. After which, Roman wrapped four of the fish sticks in a palm leaf for Summer. Daniel kicked sand over the fire to put it out and having checked they had everything; the boys made their way back to the boathouse.

With their spirits high and their bellies full, they jostled with each other, and pushed through the door. Axel touched his lips to warn the others to be quiet, then he tiptoed to the rear area of the boathouse to rouse Summer.

He looked somewhat stunned when he realised that she was not there and retreated back to the others to let them know.

"What do you mean, she's not there, she must be, are you sure?"

"Well of course I'm sure, see for yourselves."

The others went to the rear of the boat house and found no sign of Summer.

"We had better go and look for her, she must have tried to find us and got lost. One of us should stay here though, in case she comes back. Perhaps we should draw lots?"

"No need for that, I'm happy to stay here."

"Ok, Roman, we'll scout around the area outside and make our way down to the beach and back. It's a good job we found this torch earlier, we will need it out there in the dark. She can't have gone far, she's probably just lost her sense of direction in the dark and on her way back, hopefully she will see the torch and realise it's us."

11: ROMAN WAITS FOR SUMMER IN THE BOAT SHED

Told by Roman:

Axel and Daniel left the boat shed, I closed the door behind them, I was worried that something may have happened to Summer. It had been quite a long while since we had gone to catch fish. I was conscious that Summer had not eaten as her portion was still wrapped in the palm leaf.

I busied myself, making the area at the back as comfortable as possible for us all. Whilst I was doing so, I found a small piece of cloth. As I picked it up, I could smell a strange chemical scent on it. I sniffed at it more closely and reeled back feeling a little strange. I realised then that the cloth had been doused in some kind of chemical, like chloroform, that knocked people out.

The cloth was still a little damp, which suggested it had been recently used. Oh goodness, I thought, it must have been used whilst we were cooking our fish. This meant someone had taken Summer, I must alert the others. Feeling a little woozy I made my way to the door, only to find I was not alone. As I reached it, I heard the click of the outside bolt being drawn into place, closing it tight to prevent me leaving.

Concerned and angry I shouted, "Who goes there? Let me out, you have locked me in, let me out!" There was no response, just the sound of retreating footsteps. Whoever it was, had either not heard me or had deliberately ignored my plea.

I thought maybe it had been the boatman, who forgetting that he had told us to sleep in the boat shed, had absentmindedly locked up for the night. He was probably deaf, I thought, as after all he was rather old.

After a while, I became more worried about Summer, I started to think that whoever had locked me in had done it deliberately. I didn't think on this occasion, that it would have been Daniel or Axel, as they were also worried about Summer, and yet didn't know about the rag I had found.

No, it would not be them, but who could it be, it doesn't make sense. It must surely have been the boatman.

The time seemed to tick by slowly, I racked my brains as to who could have done it, but to no avail. Speaking my thoughts out loud, I said to myself.

"Not many people know we are here on the island. Only the boatman knows we're in his boat shed. Unless he has told someone but why, we don't have any money."

I turned my thoughts to how I could get out and warn the others, to also make them aware of what may have happened to Summer. I looked around the boat shed for an escape route. There was only one door, which I knew was locked. There was a window high up which if I could squeeze through it, I may be able to jump down the other side. I was sure that the drop the other side, would have a soft landing. I was aware that the boat house was close to the beach. What I wasn't sure about, was whether there were any boats laying there but pushed this thought from my head.

The only other possible access to the outside, was a small window in the roof. I was just in the process of moving a packing case across to the window, to stand on when I heard voices. "Oh, good they are back!"

I was just about to call out to them, when I sensed there was something strange about their voices. I quickly backed away from the door, then hid behind the boat. The voices came closer.

I heard one of them say, "We will have to shift him tomorrow, we can put him in the bow of the boat."

"What about the girl, what you going to do with her, she's a bit of a handful?"

"She will have to stay with you, stash her in a cavern, or somewhere well out of sight for the time being. I don't want anyone to find her until we have finished with her but mind you, don't hurt her. We've got enough trouble on our hands, and we don't want any more complication."

"Ok, I'll treat her like a princess so that she doesn't suspect anything. What you going to do with the others? They're bound to notice she is missing?"

I backed further away from the door and hid behind a crate in the corner. I could see the doorway, and if possible, could make a run for it.

I knew they wouldn't be able to catch me as I had a lightning speed that I only used when danger lurked. Otherwise, I kept my unusual ability hidden. My parents were aware of my special and unusual abilities, otherwise they were not shown or mentioned to anyone.

As I was not sure if the old man was the one who had locked me in, I thought I would keep out of sight. The light was very dim, and threw shadows across the shed, which I hoped would be to my advantage.

Expecting the men to come in and collect the boat from the boat shed I waited in anticipation for the door to open.

After what seemed like an age, though actually only a few minutes, the first voice said, “Here, give us a hand with this. If you drag the front of the trailer, I'll push from behind and we’ll soon have it afloat."

This was followed by a loud, clanging noise and some heavy breathing.

“That'll do, let's get the sail up and get it along the coast.”

“We’ll need to have it ready for him pretty sharpish if we're going to get the job done tonight. We'll have to run it down to the waters’ edge on the trailer, then set it afloat on the tide using the motor until we can get further out into the sea.”

“Hitch the dinghy up on the back, we may need it later to get back to the mainland.”

The men were working and talking oblivious to the fact that I was in the shed and could hear what they were saying. Even with the door locked and them outside, the sound penetrated through to my sensitive and excellent hearing, another of my unusual abilities.

Without attempting to unlock the boathouse, the two men had hitched a boat on its trailer and moved it in readiness to take it to the water's edge and set it afloat.

Having completed their task, they had dragged the boat down, further and further away from the boathouse, with considerable speed. I could hear the scraping sound of the trailer fading as it moved into the distance.

After approximately fifteen minutes had passed, I realised that I was safe to move from my cramped position. They were out of earshot and would not hear me moving about. I could once again try to make my escape.

I dragged the packing case into position beneath the window and climbed on top of it. I knew I would have to work fast, as I didn't know if anyone else would come to the boathouse. Not knowing who had locked it, meant I didn't know if they would suddenly return.

I climbed onto the packing case then slipped my Bowie knife from out of its case, that I held on my belt. Using it to prise the lock on the window open, I soon heard the sound of its inner workings click. Standing on tiptoe, I pushed on it hard, and it sprung open; with a bit more effort I was able to open it further to allow me to crawl through it. Slipping my knife back into its case, I swung myself through the window and dropped silently to the soft sandy beach below. Flicking on my head torch, I was able to make out the tracks that had been left in the sand when the two men had taken the boat and its trailer. They had also taken the dinghy, leaving only a small rowing boat that was upturned, half buried in the sand.

Getting my bearings, I walked in the direction of the steps taken earlier to catch the fish. I was hopeful that I would bump into the others, to be able to warn them from going back to the boat shed. Luckily, they had not had very much stuff with them, so apart from the fish I had taken back for Summer, I had managed to get everything into my backpack and brought it with me. I had found some head torches amongst the equipment in the boat house, one of which I had put on, the others I had stuffed into my bag. I had decided to eat the fish, I felt bad about that as it had been for Summer. I knew, however, that she would not be back to eat it so had decided to do so myself. I didn't want to leave it behind as it would alert someone to my presence, if they were to access the inside of the boat shed.

I could feel the fish in my tummy, not my favourite food, however sufficient to keep the wolves away from the door (an expression Mum would say to me, when she gave me a snack between meals). I hoped it would do just that, although I knew it was not real, but just a saying. I strained my ears to see if I could hear anything or anyone. All was silent, so I gave a low whistle followed by a high whistle and then another low whistle in the hope that the others would recognise it as an SOS call.

I carried on walking to where the campfire had been and repeated the whistles. I was just about to give up and retrace my steps, when I heard a reply. My whistle was being echoed. It sounded quite distant at first but gradually became louder and louder. I found a rock to hide behind in case it was a total stranger, and put my hand on my knife, ready in case of danger.

I held my breath as the sound of soft footsteps in the sand came closer and closer. Two bobbing heads and the light from a torch appeared, silhouetted by the moon, they stopped by the campfire and whistled.

"Well Axel, we have hunted everywhere for Summer, and not found her. I thought that whistle SOS may have been her, but there is no one here, so I guess not."

Roman, on hearing Daniel's voice, started to breathe, and let out a loud whistle.

"Who goes there, show yourself or I'll shoot."

"Daniel, it's ok, it's me Roman. I have been whistling the SOS signal to find you and warn you not to go back to the boathouse.

"Why ever not, we are supposed to be sleeping there tonight as soon as we have found Summer."

"That's just it we can't, you didn't find Summer because she has been kidnapped!"

"Don't be silly, who would want to kidnap her. What would be the point, she doesn't have any money or rich families, does she?"

"I know it sounds unbelievable, but it's true. As you know, when we went back to the boathouse with the fish for her, I thought she must be asleep as it was all quiet, but I was wrong, she wasn't there. Then after you left to look for her, and whilst I was looking round the boat house for her, in case she was hiding for a prank, someone locked me in. I also found a piece of cloth that's had a chemical on it, something like chloroform and it was still damp, so I guessed that whoever used it, had used it on Summer and taken her away."

"Oh! but that sounds a bit fanciful Roman, you sure you didn't fall asleep and imagine it?"

"No, of course I didn't. It is true. I was locked in. When I tried to find a way out, I was just pulling a packing case over, to use as a stepping stall under the window, when I heard voices. It was two men, so I hid because I thought they would unlock the boat house and come in and find me."

"So, did they?"

"No Axel they didn't, they pulled a boat on a trailer from beside the boat house down to the waters' edge, they took the dinghy with them also."

"So, what you worried about then?"

"I'm sorry Daniel, but I know Summer is in danger. The men were talking about smuggling some guy out in the bottom or bow of the boat tonight to move him tomorrow. They were also arranging for the girl to be hidden with him until they are finished with her. The older sounding one of the two guys gave the orders, and said she wasn't to be harmed."

"So, you see boys, to go back to the boathouse would put us in danger, and we now have to find Summer as well as the old man."

"I managed to pack all our gear into my backpack. I'm sorry, but I had to eat the fish so that they wouldn't know I had been there. I escaped through the locked window, which I opened using my Bowie knife, and came to find you."

"It's good that you did, thank you."

"I'm sorry Axel that I couldn't do so sooner."

"Well, you have certainly had an adventure whilst Axel and I have been out here looking for Summer. If we can't go back to the boat house, we will need to find somewhere to sleep tonight."

"Daniel?"

"Yes Axel"

"If we can't go back there, does that then mean we can't go back in the morning for the sea dog to take us in his boat back to Miami?"

"I guess so Axel, if Roman is right, we can't trust anyone, as we don't know who took Summer or locked the boat shed."

"What do we do now then?"

"I guess we try and find a cave for the night, and with luck find Summer at the same time."

"Oh! that's a great idea, I don't think! How are we supposed to find a cave in the dark?"

"Well Axel it's the best I can do, unless you have a better idea?"

Axel looked a bit sheepish. "No, I don't, I'm sorry Daniel, it's just this place gives me the creeps. I get bad vibes from it and sense we are in some real danger if we don't get off the island soon."

"What about you Roman? What do you think we should do?"

"Well, I think Axel is right. We are in danger here, but we can't leave while Summer is missing, so I guess you're right too, we need to find her and a cave to shelter in for the night."

"Okay, then that's what we will do, we will need to be careful as we all sense we're in danger. We will head toward the coastline and look for a cave in the rocks. There is said to be lots of caves, we just need to find the right one for us and if we're lucky we will find the one with Summer in it. Let's go!"

The boys headed off toward the more rugged part of the coastline, where the rock face jutted out toward the sea, to seek shelter for the night and find their friend

12: SUMMER ALL ALONE

Told by Summer:

Meanwhile, I was just coming around. I lay on a rough mattress of stuffed straw; a torn blanket was laid across me that did not reach my shoulders. The air was warm, although I shivered as I tried to sit up. My hands were bound with torn cotton strips of material. My legs were tied at the ankles, they were beginning to throb as I tried to move them. The circulation in my ankles had been restricted by the tight bindings and I winced at the pain. My head was also throbbing, I presumed it was what was on the cloth that had knocked me out. Feeling nauseous, I tried to raise myself onto my elbows and look around to try and identify where I was.

It was no good, I could only do it again a few minutes at a time, and as I did so my head felt like it was going to explode. From what I could see, I ascertained that this was not a person's home, garage, or even a boat shed. The walls were thick rock, the ceiling of the same rock, with damp slime patches. The ground was hard, but also covered in sand with small boulders laying about.

A rough, wooden three-legged stool was placed opposite the makeshift bed, and another placed near to the side at the top of the bed. A jug of water and chipped mug were placed on it.

After much effort to take in my surroundings, I concluded that this must be some kind of cave. Listening hard, I tried to make out the sound of the sea, but it eluded me. This, I thought, meant I was either high up in the rocks or deep within a series of caves.

Whichever it was it was unlikely anyone would come to my aid if I attempted to call out. Why are people you can trust, never around when you need them? I whispered hoarsely to myself with my throat dry and sore.

With the realisation of how cut off I was from the boys and feeling unwell and frustrated by my inability to move, tears ran down my face. Exhausted from my efforts, I lay back on to the mattress and waited for my captors to return. It wasn't long before I had drifted back off to sleep.

As the minutes and hours passed, the cave room had become colder and darker, my body much stiffer and numb from the bindings round my wrists and ankles.

I awoke, startled by the sound of voices that I did not recognise. It was two men. I could just make out their outline from the shadows. They spoke softly, but with purpose, one of them came over to me and loosened my bindings. the other one brought across a bowl of what proved to be spicy meat. Their features were indistinguishable in the darkness, and their accents were clearly not English but maybe American or Afro Caribbean, possibly disguised by them.

They shook me to make sure I was awake, then without ceremony shoved the dish of food into my now, unbound hands, and ordered me to eat.

Even though I had been untied, I had very little ability to move unaided. Realising this, they removed the bowl and pulled me to a sitting position. They returned the bowl, but not before giving me a sip of water from the jug.

When they were satisfied that I had eaten sufficiently, as well as had some water, they removed the bowl and proceeded to re-bind my hands and feet. I struggled, to prevent this, but the weakness in my body and stiff joints, prevented me from stopping them.

"If you keep still, and stop struggling, it won't hurt so much."

"Why are you doing this? I don't understand. What do you want from me?" Due to the weakness in my body, when I asked this my voice sounded strange to my ears.

"We want the professor, your friends know where he is, you will not get the treasure before us. We trade you for him, you sleep now."

"I don't want to argue, but…." I was unable to finish my sentence as the man shoved a rag in my mouth, then a chloroform-soaked rag under my nose.

Once again, Summer, drifted off into a drugged sleep.

Satisfied that she was asleep and secure, the two men left the interior of the cave and made their way out into the open.

The air was much cooler now although not cold, it was just a breeze coming from the sea that made the temperature more bearable than it has been during the daytime.

"We better contact Henry on the mainland, find out what he's learnt from that guy. It was a good ruse, when you told them, to arrest him. I bet that put the wind up him. I bet he hasn't sussed that they aren't real detectives. Serve him right though, pompous ass, thinks he can go meddling in our affairs."

The two men made their way back home, muttering to each other, what they were going to do to anyone that got in their way.

They hadn't been gone long, when Axel, Roman and Daniel stumbled on their footprints.

Axel was looking down as he was walking, watching the light from his head torch, dancing shadows on the sandy ground.

"Look guys, see here, there are footprints. They can't be ours, we're not going around in circles, are we?"

"Well, I don't think so, besides they are larger than our footprints, look, see what I mean?"

"Yes, you're right Daniel, that means we must be very close as these prints are still very clear to see."

"Yes, and they seem to be heading away from us, do you think we should follow them, or trace them back to where they start from?"

"I reckon we should trace them back, after all Roman has said that two men said they had Summer, and these are two sets of footprints. Maybe they have dumped Summer somewhere round here and gone off home".

"Oh! Surely, they can't be the same two who came to the boat house as they have not long gone off to put the boat out on the tide, with the old guy in the bottom of it. They must have accomplices."

"Gosh that's tricky, that makes it harder to know who is behind it and what they want."

"We don't even know if they are working together or not. Why would they take Summer? It doesn't make any sense if they already have the old guy."

"You're right Axel, it's a bit odd, perhaps they are different men which means there may be more of them, and possibly a larger gang."

"I still think we should trace them back, this place as you know, is riddled with caves which you can probably see in daylight. We may find Summer and another cave to hide in for the night. The weather is building up into a storm, and we are going to need shelter."

"Come on then, before this wind gets stronger and blows the sand across the footprints."

The boys turned their attention to retracing the footprints that they had found. Buffeted by the wind, they carefully followed each other. They shone their torches downward to help distinguish the tracks from the shadows, thrown by the waving of palm trees.

It wasn't long before Daniel put his hand up to signify stop. Putting his fingers across his mouth to signify silence, he pointed toward the opening of a cave. A dim light was glowing inside it. The boys switched off their torch and slowly stepped inside the cave. Ears straining, they listened for voices or something to signify that they were not alone.

On hearing nothing, Daniel waved them forward and they inched their way into the cave. Gradually, their eyes grew accustomed to the light within the cave. The smell of the sea and rotted fish within the sandy floor, made them hold their noses until they were far enough in for it to have dissipated.

The deeper they went, the narrower the space became within. Soon, they reached what they initially took to be the end of the cave. The darkness was greater, but as they put a hand forward and raised their head torches, they realised it was an entrance to a number of smaller caves and tunnels.

"Oh drat, now what do we do? We can't go down them all at once!"

"Don't worry, I have an idea. If we take them one at a time and mark the way as we go, we will find our way back and be able to go down the next one. That way, we can listen for anyone coming behind or ahead of us. What do you think?"

"A good idea Roman."

"How about if we whistle first, to see if anyone whistles back! After all Summer knows the signal and may answer."

"Well, yes Axel, but we don't know if anyone is down there with her, and we don't want to alert them, do we?"

"I guess not Daniel."

"Come on then, we will take the one on the left first."

The boys followed Daniel as they travelled deeper into the cave, and for once, luck was on their side. They were able to reach the end without meeting any strangers. They were just about to turn around and retrace their way back to the other cave entrances, when Daniel sensed that they were not alone.

He could not see anyone at first, but after crouching down on the floor, he could make out a form, laying there. Signalling to the other two to come closer, quietly, he moved closer to the strange looking shape. He put out his hand to touch it and snatched it away, reeling backwards.

"What is it Daniel?" whispered the other two simultaneously.

"I don't know, it was all cold and clammy, yet familiar in shape."

"What do you mean?"

"Well, I think it was an arm, do you think it could be a dead body?"

"Let me see" Roman pushed past Daniel and stretched out his arm until he could reach the form, "Ugh, I think maybe you're right!"

"Oh, I do hope it's not Summer's dead body, quick shine your torch on it one of you!"

Roman and Daniel shone their torches on the form and could clearly make out the shape of a body. Axel was right, it was Summer, and she was laying still, bound and gagged on the floor.

Daniel bent over her and felt her pulse, she was alive, but either still drugged or very near death.

"Quick you two, help me get these ropes off her and carry her out into the open."

Roman pulled out his Bowie knife for the second time that

evening and cut through the bindings round her feet and ankles. Daniel pulled the rag from her mouth and with Axel's help, lifted her onto his shoulder.

With his immense strength, he managed to carry Summer to the entrance of the cave. Axel went ahead and Roman behind, to ensure that if anyone appeared, they would be able to protect Daniel and Summer. Roman held his knife at the ready and Axel had Daniel's gun, held out in front of him, ready to use if necessary.

They were, however, able to make their way out unheeded to find safe cover nearby. They lay Summer down on the sand and started to rub her limbs, to get her circulation going and warm her up.

"If only we had a hot drink or something to give her, to bring her round."

"Maybe we can carry her back to the other bay where those food places were. There may be something we can find that's still open, a night club or something."

"We will have to take turns to carry her. It's not fair if Daniel has to use all his strength to do so."

"If only there was someone on the island, we could ask to help us."

"Perhaps there is, but we need to move fast, before the men who abducted her, come back."

The boys stripped off their shirts and wrapped them round Summer as best they could. Then between them, they carried her back toward the quay they had arrived at that morning.

It seemed a long time since they had arrived. They were feeling tired and hungry, worried that they would be stranded on the island for days, too afraid to ask for help.

The storm had increased, with flashes of lightning and rumbles of thunder. Rain poured down and the humidity grew more intense. Sweat poured off the boys as they carried their burden.

13: THE BOYS GO FOR HELP

Unbeknown to them, Jethro, who had shown Summer round the island earlier that day, was sitting in a bar thinking about Summer, and how he had grown quite fond of her whilst they had wandered in and out of the market stools.

He sat thinking about how she had fallen on the quay, and felt a little pang of guilt, for causing the accident. He recalled how thankful she had been for his help and how innocent. He had not enjoyed taking advantage of her, but it had been necessary.

It had taken a while to shake off the boy. He sensed he did not trust him, and therefore could scupper his plans. He needed to gain her trust, to enable her support with finding the professor. Little did she know that he had overheard her plans that she made on the boat. He had no knowledge of how the other two boys had spent their day. Although he did not wish to include them in his quest, he admired their courage and fortitude.

Jethro continued to mull over the day's happenings and his part in them. He sat and wondered where the children would have found transport back to the mainland.

Whilst Jethro was sitting thinking of Summer, Roman was also mulling over the day's activities. It had been a strange day, with meeting new friends, going on a boat trip adventure, exploring the island. He had missed Summer, even though she was a girl, she had been good company.

He was worried about her, even though she had been brave, as well as clever, making sure that he did not let Jethro know about their plans.

Maybe he had misjudged Jethro, after all, he had helped them and brought Summer back to the quay side safely for the boat, albeit a bit late. Perhaps he could help them now? Roman mulled this over in his mind for a while. He was torn and struggled to decide, as on the one hand he did not trust Jethro, but on the other, he could not positively say he had deliberately done them any harm.

"You're very quiet Roman, you okay?"

"Yeah sure, it's just that I was thinking, I know this sounds crazy, but we need to find some-one to help us, and Jethro came to mind."

"What? The guy that tripped Summer up on the gangway! You must be kidding."

"I said it sounded crazy Daniel, because none of us really trust him, but he did help Summer after he picked her up, and he showed us round the island without any trouble."

"Okay, Roman, that's true, maybe we misjudged him. What do you think Axel?"

"Well, I think Roman's right, none of us trust him, not even

Summer, so that must tell us something. I'm not sure it's a good idea, but maybe we can put him to the test. We must be on our guard though and watch what we say when we are within earshot of him. The question is how are we going to find him? He may have gone back to the mainland."

"No, I don't think so, he said he was here on vacation all week. He likes the night clubs and bars, so maybe he is in one of them."

"Well, I don't know about you guys, but I got a strange sense of danger whenever he was close by, so maybe we will seek him out that way. We will have to find some help soon if we're going to help Summer."

The boys agreed that they would seek out Jethro, to ask him to help Summer. They needed somewhere warm for her, and maybe a doctor.

"We can't carry her too far in this storm, perhaps it would be best if I go ahead and see if I can find him and bring him back here. Maybe Axel, you should stay with her, and Roman come with me, as you will recognise Jethro and he you?

"Sure, that sounds like a good idea if Axel is okay with it. How about we use the whistle to signal when we are back, or if in any trouble?"

"That's a great idea, what say you Axel?"

"It sounds good to me, you had better be off. Be as quick as you can, good luck!"

Daniel and Roman, feeling satisfied that they had left Summer with

Axel, both comfortable and hidden well, left the shelter.

They took turns in using their torches, to save the batteries as much as possible.

Daniel led the way at first, then they walked side by side as the track they followed widened out.

They headed toward the built-up area of the island, where Roman and Summer had been with Jethro earlier that day.

"If we're lucky, we will find him in a bar."

Having reached their destination, feeling somewhat tired and thirsty, they searched various bars. After having a couple of drinks, however they were unable to find Jethro. Roman was convinced that he was on the island somewhere. "Let's try some of the local huts that are rented out to island visitors, maybe he is in one of them."

This proved to be more successful, although not before they wound up in trouble with some of the residents. Most of whom were trying to weather the storm, and not happy to be disturbed by a couple of youngsters asking questions. One man became so enraged, that he sent Daniel reeling backwards, from a massive blow from his fist. Daniel fell flat on his back catching his head on a rock, from which made him see stars. His legs felt numb initially then painful, probably from the bruising to his back as he hit the ground.

Roman helped him to his feet, and as Daniel was unsteady and feeling dizzy, Roman looked around for something that Daniel could use to help him lean on to walk more steadily.

"I knew this was a bad idea, you may recall I said so. I knew this would end in trouble."

Roman turned to look at him, he saw he was barely standing, he had blood running down his face, from his nose where he was punched, with more running down his back from his head wound. Roman didn't think he could argue with Daniel as he had proved his point, so he just smiled and gave him a peculiar shaped stick to use as a support.

"Come Daniel, let's move away from here, it's too dangerous. We have already upset one guy, we can't be sure the people who abducted the old man or Summer, aren't hanging around this area. Let's see if we can find somewhere to rest, and a doctor of some sort to dress those wounds. Maybe we could get them to help Summer as well. What way do you think we should head now?"

When his friend didn't answer, he repeated the question, but Daniel didn't respond. Thinking this strange, Roman turned to look at Daniel and was shocked to find that he was standing as if in a trance. "Daniel what is it, are you ok, you look like you have seen a ghost, can you hear me Daniel?"

Roman touched his friend gently on the shoulder, then gave him a little shake repeating his question. After a few seconds, which to Roman felt like hours, Daniel shook his head as if he was just waking up, then turned toward his friend, "Sorry Roman, did you say something?"

"Well yes, are you alright? Only you looked a bit strange, you didn't seem to hear me?"

"Yes, I'm fine, I don't know why, but when I stood up and leant on that old stick, I had the strangest sensation. It was as if I was back holding the professor's hand, or rather him holding mine. I also felt as if my father was trying to contact me or warn me in some way."

"You sure you are alright? You don't think that maybe that punch and bang on the head gave you a bit of concussion, do you?"

"Maybe, maybe not, anyhow I'm fine now, so let's find someone to help us."

Daniel, with the support of the stick, led the way and the boys resumed their search for Jethro. They were unaware at the time, that Summer had come out of her drugged state sufficiently for Axel to explain what had happened and where the others had gone. Neither were they aware, that Summer was able to explain what events she could remember and confirm that Jethro had not been amongst her captors.

Axel was relieved to hear that Jethro was not one of the captors. He had been worried that he would put the others in danger. He also tried to work out how many people could have known the reason for their visit to the island. He knew that their parents knew they were coming, but not what they planned to do when they arrived. They could not have overheard them speaking about it on the boat as they were not with them.

Jethro was on the boat, but they had not spoken to anyone else who was. They spoke to the people at the paper, but they were not on the boat. They had spoken to the ferry boat captain, but not about their plans. They had spoken to the boat shed owner, but only to seek passage on his boat back to the mainland.

It struck Axel that he had not asked Summer if the boat shed owner had been one of the people who had abducted her. Realising that she probably needed more time to relax from her ordeal, to feel more herself, rather than struggling with the after effects of the drugs she had been given; before she would be strong enough to talk about her experience, he decided to wait until the others returned before asking any more questions.

Summer lay watching Axel, trying to work him out. He appeared to be a quiet thoughtful boy. It struck her that although he had come on the boat with them, she had not had much opportunity to chat to him or get to know him. He had after all been Daniel's friend, and not at the first meeting at the airport where she had met Daniel. She looked at him now, he appeared to be of a similar age to them, she guessed thirteen or fourteen, he had short brown hair and his skin was sort of tanned and smooth, a bit like the holiday makers. He seemed a serious type though, good humoured, he fell in with their plans without any fuss.

Summer decided that she liked what she saw and thought she could trust him, that he would do his best to keep them safe. She wanted to ask him what had been happening whilst she had been trapped in the cave, but the waves of exhaustion from pain in her ankles and wrists, made her feel too weak to strike up a conversation. Instead, she just hugged herself to keep warm, and watched him through drooping eyelids.

The two of them sat in silence for a while, both lost in their own thoughts. They were brought out of it by a sudden gust of wind and streak of lightning followed by a clap of thunder. Summer shivered and screamed, before she realised what had happened. Axel turned to her, calmly soothing her panic.

"It's ok Summer, you're quite safe, it won't be long before the others are back, and we will find shelter for the night"

"But why can't we go back to the boat shed?"

"Why? Well, we don't know if the owner was involved in your abduction. He could have been one of the men that took you or arranged it to happen."

"Oh, but I don't think he was, at least I don't remember hearing him!"

"You may be right, but I'm not sure we can trust your memory as they drugged you to make you sleep. He may have come in during those times."

"Oh dear, I do hope not, he was going to take us back to the mainland. I want to go home, I don't like this island anymore." Tears ran down her face. She swiped her arm across them to try and wipe them off. Axel turning to her, comforted her again and reassured her that all would be ok.

Unaware of Daniel's injuries, Axel convinced himself that help would arrive soon, and they would be back at the hotel before breakfast tomorrow.

He started to think about his parents, he loved them dearly, and knew that he was a constant worry to them. His happy go lucky attitude and behaviour tended to get him into trouble, and he had promised them that he would behave well on this holiday. They didn't realise how serious and reserved he could be.

He was more thoughtful, deep and mature than they realised. He kept this side of him hidden most of the time. It had come to the surface when his parents had introduced him to Daniel's family at the table, and vice versa. He did not wish to show them up or make a fool of himself in front of Daniel. He didn't always remember to do as asked, but this was not malicious or intentional, but rather due to lack of concentration and listening.

He had a good imagination and was always coming up with little ideas for inventions, he used lateral thinking (by this I mean he could think outside of the box). He could also see patterns of things, in music, papers, behaviours etc. Even though he wore glasses for reading, his long sight was exceptional, and he would register much of what he saw and memorise it.

It was this skill that Axel was tapping into whilst sitting with Summer. His mind was wandering back to the visit to the newspaper.

The reception they had received there on arrival was a bit strange. The lady had been very nice to them. A bit like his Mum would have been. The man, however, seemed to be friendly one minute, then angry and not very nice or patient. Even though Axel was not part of most of the conversation, he could pick up a level of hostility toward them.

He had watched the newspapers being printed and seen news headlines about the professor, that emphasised his missing staff. Axel was able to ascertain from this that the staff was a historic artefact, not a group of people. This artefact was deemed in myth to have special powers that could present a risk to people if it fell into the wrong hands. The paper also mentioned priceless artefacts that were missing, but these were not specified.

Axel started to think maybe they were not the only ones at risk on this island. He recalled that Daniel and himself had not had an opportunity to discuss their visit to the newspaper, neither had they relayed any of their findings to Summer or Roman. He became anxious to do this, as he believed that there was a clue to achieving their quest hidden within the information that they all held.

He was startled out of his thoughts by another loud clap of thunder, and cry from Summer. He was about to turn to her, when he realised there was another sound coming from the undergrowth.

"Quick Summer, turn that torch off and keep quiet, someone's coming!"

Summer held her breath, too afraid to breath in case she screamed. The rustling sound got louder, and soft thud of footsteps came closer. Then came a whistling sound that was repeated three times. Axel switched on the torch and saw Roman and Daniel followed by a dark, skinned man.

Summer on seeing who it was, dragged herself across on wobbly legs, and collapsed at his feet, saying, "Daniel, it's you, but your hurt!"

Daniel smiled at her and replied, "Yes, but it was worth it to see you awake."

Turning to Axel he said, "Sorry we took so long, we didn't find Jethro but we found a doctor. This is Dr Mombassa. He will check Summer to make sure she is ok and dress any wounds she may have from her bindings."

Axel looked at Daniel as he came closer and further into the light, "You're hurt Daniel, what happened?"

"Oh, it's nothing, just a head wound, we will tell you all about it later, as soon as the doc here has checked out Summer and we have shared some of his wife's Jerk chicken. "

Axel nodded absentmindedly, he was not really taking much notice, his attention was drawn to the odd shaped stick that Daniel was leaning on. He had a recollection of having seen it before somewhere. He opened his mouth to speak but was unceremoniously brushed aside before he could say anything, by the large dark, skinned doctor, who appeared to be mumbling mambo jumbo.

"Is he a witch doctor?"

Roman and Daniel both laughed, "Why no Axel, although we both thought so at first!"

"What's he saying then?"

"It's a chant. He is a spiritual healer that uses his spiritual powers, as well as herbs, which he makes into potions. Don't worry, he has also trained as a proper medical doctor in Miami, we have seen his certificates."

"We were lucky to find him, as he knows about drugs and how to treat people who have taken them or been given them."

Whilst this conversation was going on, Summer was being examined. Mombo, as the doctor called himself, was checking stiff joints, eyes, pulse and general physical appearance. Soon he turned around to the others and his serious face turned into a big smile, with his white teeth beamed across his dark skin. "Food and water and a warm bed, and she'll be as right as rain tomorrow."

"But where are we going to find that tonight? The only thing we do have is rain."

"Oh Axel, you are funny, Mombo here has offered to let us stay at his hut tonight and his wife is making us Jerk chicken, whilst we speak. By taking it in turns, we can carry Summer there, but we must be careful so as not to arouse the attention of strangers on our way."

Dr Mombo turned to Axel, looking embarrassed, "My sincere apologies for making you think I was a witch doctor. I hope I didn't frighten you, please forgive me?" He held his hand out to Axel.

Looking contrite and embarrassed himself, Axel shook hands with Mombo, then smiled.

"I'm sorry, I didn't mean to appear rude or ungrateful for your presence, thank you for your help."

"I'm sorry to interrupt you two, but if we don't get a move on, we will all be in danger of being seen by Summers' attackers."

"Sorry Daniel," they responded in unison, "We're coming."

Arrangements were then made for taking turns in carrying Summer to the Doctor's hut. Daniel was not allowed to take a turn due to his injuries, and therefore resumed his place at the front of the little party, using his strange stick as a support. The Doctor walked alongside him, giving directions.

As he leant on the stick, Daniel felt the strange feeling come over him as before. It was as if the professor was holding his hand drawing him forward, whilst a message was coming through from his father, to beware of strangers, trust no one.

The little group moved slowly and carefully, tracking through the undergrowth and along sandy beaches until they could slip unseen into Mombo's hut. The two boys had crossed their arms and held hands to form a chair for Summer. They struggled to make good progress this way, so had changed to giving her a piggyback. Summer was heavy, as not able to hold her own weight. After a while, she slipped off Roman's back onto the sand, feeling exhausted and embarrassed by her weakness, she wept floods of tears. Mombo turned, and seeing her distress and the boy's tired faces, he walked back and lifted her up into his arms and carried her the rest of the way.

As they entered the warm room of the little hut, with its smell of jerk chicken coming from the stove, their spirits rose. Even Summer forgot for a moment her worries about not getting back to the mainland.

Little did the children know, that chaos was occurring back at the hotel.

14: CONCERN BACK AT THE MIAMI HOTEL

It had been some time since Daniel's father had been arrested. The little group of parents had continued to chat over their coffee after he had gone, expecting him to return within the hour. When he did not, and the children did not return for dinner as expected, they became very concerned.

Daniel's mother once again took control of the situation, "This is ridiculous! You must know where he is if your people arrested him?" she was talking loudly into the hotel phone with the desk sergeant of the Miami Police. Her frustration was clear in her voice. "If you can't help me, then put me through to someone who can. There must be a senior detective there who knows, surely, and be quick about it."

The rest of the parents stood nearby, listening to her give instructions to the person on the other end of the phone. Summer and Axel's mothers were also distressed and anxious, as the children hadn't returned for their meal as expected. Unclear as to why they had chosen to go to the islands, not knowing if they had gone on a wild goose chase, or just thinking it an adventure, both mothers were worried some mishap may have occurred to make them miss the boat back. Their husbands were also worried, but tried to reassure their wives that all would be okay.

"As I keep telling you ma'am, we don't have any detectives of that name in this precinct. I can get the president himself down here, who will tell you the same. You must either have their names wrong, or they are from some other area detective agency. Now, if there is nothing else I can help you with, I will bid you goodbye."

The phone clicked at the other end. As Daniel's mother was about to mention the children being missing, assumed, to be stranded on the islands, the line went dead.

"Well, I never, how rude of him to cut me off, the insolent little man was most unhelpful." Turning to the others, she threw her arms up in the air in frustration. "He reckons that they don't have detectives named Brown or Green. They have no record of Arthur being arrested. He said I must be mistaken or have the wrong precinct or detective agency."

Flopping into a chair, she called for the waiter, "Please bring a fresh jug of coffee as well as an area phone book." Determined, not to be put off, she took it from the coffee tray as soon as it arrived. Franticly, she scrolled through it and rang every detective agency she could find as well as every police department. Sipping her coffee between calls, she then jotted down the name of the agency and worker she had spoken to, in case she needed to get back to them later.

The minutes ticked by, with no positive results. Worried about her husband, Daniel's mother decided that he was probably able to look after himself. It was now time to concentrate on getting help in finding the children. Changing tack, she scrolled through the phone book again. On finding the number for the boat trip company, she made a number of calls to see if she could track down the one the children had used. Roman and Axel's mothers helped with the calls and each number was recorded, helpful or unhelpful.

The outcome, however, was that the ferries were not running again until the next day. That the passenger lists were filed away and kept confidential in a locked cupboard.

They would, therefore, have to call back the next day, to provide evidence that they were legally entitled to the information.

In an attempt to get some help, Roman's father contacted the police. He believed that as a man, he would receive a more positive response. He explained to the desk sergeant of the local Miami police station, that the children had gone off on the ferry boat that morning however had not returned. In addition to which, two men posing as detectives, had come and arrested one of the children's fathers, who hasn't returned either.

The desk sergeant explained that there was nothing he could do. As none of them had been missing for 24 hours, he could not file a missing person's concern claim. He suggested therefore that they call back the following day, if they have not returned.

Feeling frustrated, Roman's father thanked the desk sergeant and warned him that they would be filing a complaint. "Woe betide him, if any harm came to the missing children and parent." He took the sergeant's details for his record, and gave his own contact details, should the sergeant hear any news of the children, or their father in the meantime.

Roman's father returned to the others and had to admit that he had been mistaken. He had not managed to gain any help from the police either.

After a short while, mulling over what they could do, Axel's father decided that they would need to take the initiative and hunt down these bogus men. This may then, also lead them to the children.

"Listen everyone, we can't just sit here, we need to do something. The police are not going to help us, not before they have been missing for twenty-four hours, therefore we need to take the matter into our own hands and try to find Arthur."

"At last, a good idea, thank you Stefan for offering to help find Arthur."

"Well, I think we have to start somewhere, the police aren't going to help, at least not before tomorrow and that may be too late."

"But what about the children? They could be stranded anywhere on the island, my wife here, is upset and anxious that no one is looking for them."

"I'm sorry Jed, I hadn't forgotten about the children, and I'm not surprised Rebecca is worried silly about Summer, I'm sure we are all worried about each of the children. The problem is we do not have access to the island, or even know for sure which one they are on. To try and look for them in this storm that they have reported on the news, could put everyone in danger. No, I think we should contact the Bahama Police and ask them to try and find them and keep them safe until we can collect them."

"But what if they refuse?"

"Well Rebecca, if they do, then we will have to hire a private detective, but don't let's get ahead of ourselves, it may not come to that. Let's face it, they may have just missed the boat and rented a room for the night. They could turn up unscathed in the morning, full of excitement from their adventure."

"That's all very well, but where do we start, we don't know whether the police were real or bogus. They said they were from the Miami detective agency, but according to the police desk sergeant, there were no detectives of that name in the precinct, and we tried all the others in the book."

"First of all, can anyone remember what they looked like? Maybe, if we could draw a photo fit, then we could take it to the police station to see if they recognise them. After all, they may just have used a bogus name. If that doesn't work, we could try any fancy-dress places, or actors' agencies."

"I remember that they both had dark hair, oh, and one had a beard."

"Well done, Annalisa! Does anyone remember if they had any distinguishing features or tattoo, or anything, even glasses?"

"Yes! the one with the beard had a large ring on his right hand,

and a gold chain round his neck. His shirt was open at the neck, it looked like there was probably a medallion or something on the chain."

"Thanks Stefan, that's helpful, anything else?"

"Well yes, they both had guns in a holster under their jackets, and identical black suits."

"I remember the one with the beard was the shorter of the two, by about three inches. He was probably about five foot eight, he was more stocky too."

"Thanks, Selena, do you remember any other differences?"

"Yes, he spoke with an accent, Latin American or Mexican."

"That's really good everyone. We have quite a lot of information about the bearded guy, can anyone remember any more about the other one?"

"Well, he was taller and slimmer, with big feet. He was smarter, both in his dress and his speech."

"That's right, Rebecca, I didn't like his eyes though, they were translucent blue and cruel."

"No Annalisa, neither did I, he gave me the creeps. "

"Well, that's pretty good, we have something to go on. Can anyone here draw, so we can do a photo fit picture of them both?"

"Tobias here can draw, can't you Tobias?"

"Well, I guess I could draw a couple of sketches from what you have said, then maybe we can fill in a few more details from our memories. I'll have to get some paper and pens. It will take a little while."

"Okay, then why don't we split up, get something to eat from the supper bar, then change into something more comfortable whilst Tobias does the same, and draws the sketches. Then we can regroup here in about an hour, because I guess it's going to be a long night."

"Yes, we will have to put the finishing touches to the sketches, then split up and trawl the streets, checking different agencies, to see if anyone recognises them."

"Jean, if you have a photo of Arthur with you, perhaps you could bring that also."

"I have a small one in my purse. Will that do Stefan?"

"Sure, that will be fine."

With the suggestion agreed to by all, they left the lounge and went for their evening meal, then to their separate rooms to change as suggested.

Tobias was a little anxious, he was good at drawing and painting, but he was worried about doing a photo fit. What if he made a mistake, and they looked for the wrong people? They could all have got the details confused. He agonised over it for a good few minutes, then got the paper and pencils and sat down to draw.

After a number of attempts, he managed to get the pictures to at least reflect the details everyone had provided. He couldn't say he was happy or pleased with his drawings, he hoped however that they would be sufficient for the purpose.

"Have you finished yet Tobias, I do hope so. I am anxious to find Arthur and the children. This was supposed to be a holiday, but so far it seems to have been a nightmare. Surely someone must know where these men are, and why they have taken Arthur?"

"I'm sorry darling, it hasn't been much fun so far, but I'm sure we will be able to sort this out and get back to enjoying our holiday."

"Oh! I do hope so Tobias."

"Come Annalisa, I have finished these sketches, let's go and find the others. The sooner we start the sooner we finish."

They left the room and made their way down to the lounge. The others were ready and waiting, anxious to get started.

"Here are the sketches, please add anything you think you remember, then we can split up."

Each of them looked at the sketches and congratulated Tobias on his efforts. A few minor changes were made, such as the thickness of lips and widths of eyebrows.

As Arthur was missing, it was agreed that his wife Jean would stay at the hotel. This would mean she would be there if he returned in their absence. It would also mean she would be there if the children returned. Not too happy about this, but realising the sense in doing so, Jean agreed to the plan.

Tobias and Analisa took one of the sketches, the one of the taller of the two to show to the people at the police stations and taxi ranks. Selena and Stefan took the other one, to show to people on the streets. Rebecca and Jed opted to try the local hotels, using just the photo of Arthur, whilst the others tried the police stations and taxi ranks.

15: ARTHUR'S ORDEAL

Whilst they were all busy sorting this out, little did they know that Arthur was sat tied to a chair. His arms bound behind his back and ankles tied together. He had a bruise on his face just under his left eye and a cut lip.

"Well now, I ask you again, where is he? Where you stashed him?" The tall man grabbed Arthur's hair and pulled his head back, then let it go in anticipation of an answer.

"Where did who go, I don't know what or who you are talking about?"

He received another blow to the head from the man's fist. "Don't give me that, I ain't fooling around, you put him in a taxi and sent him some place, now where was it?"

"I've told you, I sent him to the Miami Beach hotel, which is where his room was booked. I don't know any more than you as to where he went after that."

"Did he have his staff with him?"

"No, he had no-one with him, I told you that he was complaining that his staff were missing."

"What do you mean, did he have more than one then?"

"I don't know, he didn't say."

"He just kept saying his staff was missing, then collapsed, and when he came round, he said he couldn't find his staff and asked my son to help him. I don't know any more than that. Trust me if I knew, I would tell you. But I don't, I had never met him before and had only just landed at the airport when I did. If he hadn't have collapsed in front of us at the baggage elevator, I wouldn't have given him another look."

[The phone rang,]

"Hello, yes, you sure, why? No! I'm not questioning your decision, yes ok right away."

The short guy put the phone down and signalled to his partner, the need to talk to him in private.

The tall man turned to Arthur, "Right you, don't go away" then he gave a menacing laugh, knowing full well that Arthur was tied, hand and foot, and to the chair. He joined the other guy, and they left the room, closing the door.

"Ok, what is it, who was on the phone?"

"It was the boss man, apparently things are hotting up! People have been contacting the police, wanting them to find the guy in there. Complaints have gone into the Chief of Police, and he ain't happy. Our guy on the inside is getting yellow bellied and wants out, unless we release the guy in there. The boss man says to patch him up, give him some grub, then get rid of him."

"What, do him in and dump him?"

"No idiot, thank him for his help and information, explain that we were acting on information received that we now know to be false, then put him in a cab back to his hotel."

"You're joking, aren't you?"

"No, it's no joke, the boss says to sort it out and get shot of him. Like I said, so that there is no impact on the police force. He doesn't want no hassle with him, or his inside guy."

"It don't make no sense, can't we just kill him and dump him in the lake?"

"No! If we don't do it as the boss man says, he says he won't pay us, so get on with it and hurry up."

The tall guy, muttering to himself, 'it makes no sense', over and over, with a shrug of the shoulders, turned on his heel and went back into the room.

Arthur looked up at the sound of him coming back into in the room. The guy looked mean and insolent, and Arthur wondered what pain he would inflict on him this time. He was obviously the tall guy when the short one came into the room and stood beside him.

The short one smiled at Arthur and appeared apologetic in manner.

"We are very sorry to say that a mistake has been made, and you were arrested due to information received. We now know this information was false, therefore you are free to go."

Arthur was stunned by what he heard.

"What do you mean? I have been put through all this questioning and abuse because you were misinformed? You call yourselves detectives, don't you check your information first?"

"We are very sorry sir, but we were acting on orders." said the little guy, echoed by his companion. "Yeah, acting on orders."

"So, what's your orders now, then?"

"Well sir, we aim to release you, but first we'll get you some food and drink, then when you're rested well, put you in a cab and send you back to your hotel. No harm done, eh?"

"We don't want no trouble, mate, we're just acting on orders."

"So, you were just acting on orders, were you? You put me through all that cruel interrogation. With no legal representation. You tell me it was all a mistake, and you don't want no trouble"

"Yeah, that's, right"

"Who's order?"

"The boss."

"Yes, but who's the boss?"

"We don't know, he sends messages by phone via someone else. He don't want any trouble, neither do we."

"Well, if he thinks I'm going to forget this, then he's mistaken."

Arthur was about to say that he would hunt him down and drag him, yelling and screaming through the courts, when he realised that he was in a vulnerable position at the mercy of these two guys. Given that he was still tied up to a chair, it seemed more sensible to go along with them, at least until after he had returned to the hotel. He didn't think it would take much for the tall one to turn nasty and ignore his bosses' orders.

With that in mind, he smiled. "Well, I thought you were going to set me free from here and give me something to eat. I'm starving and would have missed dinner at the hotel."

"No hard feelings then?"

"No, no hard feelings, after all you were only following orders, eh?"

"Yeah, that's right, following orders, foods coming up right away."

With that, the short guy disappeared through the door, and the tall one stood over Arthur, whilst muttering swear words to himself. He slowly undid the rope round Arthur's wrists and ankles, leaving the one around his waist that tied him to the chair until the last. Just as he did so, the little guy came back in the room.

"Here, it's no feast, but it's better than nothing" he said, as he dumped a tray on Arthur's lap.

Arthur looked at the plate on the tray. It held a chunk of ham, two fried eggs plus a slice of bread. In addition to which, was a cup of steaming hot coffee.

He smiled his thanks and tucked into the food, whilst the two guys hovered over him.

[The phone rang again].

This time the tall guy answered it. "Yeah, he's still here, what's the rush?" The voice on the other end must have sounded agitated as the tall guy looked rattled. "We are following orders, he's just finishing his food, and he'll be out of here."

The voice on the other end boomed down the phone, "Make it snappy, get rid of him. I need you here, you can drop him at his hotel on the way but be quick about it."

"Right away boss, we're on it, cab straight away."

Click - The line went dead.

Turning to his companion he said, "The boss says we got to get this guy out of here now, right now, to go get a cab and be quick. He ain't happy, somethings going down at the station, and there's notices all over the precinct."

The tall guy disappeared again, soon to return with a yellow cab. They bundled Arthur into it and mumbled something to the driver. Soon, Arthur was being whizzed through the streets on a very roundabout route, then dumped on the sidewalk close to the hotel.

Arthur is released:

I stood staring at the taxi as it pulled away. I shook my head in disbelief, why hadn't the taxi dropped me at my hotel door, after all there was no other traffic blocking his path? Could this be what had happened to the old guy? Had he been just dumped on the sidewalk then become confused and wandered around lost?

I was glad, I wasn't confused like the old guy.

I started to think about what he had been through, after comparing my taxi journey to the one the old man had endured.

I, at least, knew that my captors would have done me in but were overruled. The small guy had given the instructions to the taxi driver, maybe it was his intention to prevent any trace on the taxi being identifiable when I arrived, after all, he was only following orders. He probably didn't want to be captured himself or give any information deliberately or accidently as that could bring the police down on them. His boss wouldn't like it and wouldn't hesitate to kill them.

I shrugged my shoulders and pulled my jacket collar up, confused and angry. I rubbed my chin then winced. I could feel it was swollen from my beating. I made my way to the hotel foyer, slipped inside and up the back stairs, to try and avoid anyone seeing me. On reaching my room, I cautiously tried the door handle. It was locked. I knocked, expecting Jean to open it, but she didn't appear. Feeling even more confused and angry, I thought she must be asleep or ignoring me.

I reached into my jacket inside pocket and pulled out a key. It was a flat card key, the type I hated, why couldn't they be like the British and have a proper metal key? I thought. Having slid the card key into the thing at the side of the door, it released the door catch. I admitted to myself that it was a much quieter process than a metal key in the door. Maybe that's why they used them in the states. Perhaps over here, they were always sneaking in late at night.

I tiptoed in and peeped into the bedroom, there was no sign of Jean, my wife. I tried Daniel's room, but he was absent also. Feeling even more angry and confused, I returned to the living room area and went over to the drinks safe, like a small fridge. Taking out a miniature bottle of brandy, I opened it, slung the lid on the table and drank the liquid down. Coughing from the burning effects of it, as it hit my throat. The liquid warmed me through and calmed me a little.

Seeing my reflection in a mirror, whilst drinking the brandy, I noticed how dishevelled and dreadful I looked. My eyes were all puffy, my cheeks swollen, and mouth bloodied and bruised. My clothes were all crumpled and dirty and reflected the bad treatment I had received.

As it was quiet and no one around to disturb, I slipped out of my dirty clothes and into the shower. The hot steamy water felt heavenly on my back, reducing some of the tension in my shoulders and soothing my bruises. After drying myself, I put on some jogging bottoms and a T shirt. I took another bottle of brandy from the fridge safe and phoned room service to order a pot of coffee. I then dropped into the chair and this time sipped my brandy whilst waiting for my coffee.

It wasn't long before I had dropped off to sleep. My sleep, however, was disturbed by thoughts of being interrogated. Men peering into my face, demanding answers, these thoughts were mixed with a sense of danger and the need to get a message to Daniel. Trust no-one, kept running through my mind. This, occasionally interrupted by the face of the old man with his beard coiled round Daniel's hands.

The thumping on the door and voice calling "Room service!" brought me out of my sleep. Shaking myself awake, I called to the voice, "Coming!" I walked to the door and took the tray from the porter, then gave him a tip and closed the door again. Retreating to my position in the armchair, I put the coffee tray on a side table and sat down. My mind was in a turmoil, full of questions, such as where was my wife? what about the children, are they safe? who was the old man, why had he gone missing?

I switched on the TV news. Various statements ran across the screen.

'Elderly Professor still missing'. No news as to his whereabouts.'

'Four children reported missing, believed to be stranded on islands. Police unable to help as it's not been 24 hours since they left their hotel.'

'Holiday, makers seek answers to whereabouts of missing children and husband. They are not believed to be together.'

'Storm hits islands, unexpected weather, residents take shelter, no casualties reported yet. Miami beach residents advised to stay off beach for next 24 hours. Coast guards alerted and standing by in case needed.'

The rest of the news and weather reports continued.

I sat back in the chair and pressed the remote to turn off the TV. I reclined the armchair and sat waiting for my wife to return. It was not long before I had fallen asleep again.

The Bogus detectives are given orders:

Unknown to Arthur, the two men who had interrogated him were arguing with each other. The tall guy, Bernardo, (usually known as Berni) was telling the short guy, Max (short for Maximillian,) that they should have ditched Arthur by killing him and burying his body.

He could, after all, recognise them at any time and blab about them to the police.

Max, however, being the shorter of the two, but also the

brighter of the two, disagreed, "We don't want murder on our hands. We not getting paid for that, besides, I'm not taking the fall for no one. We were carrying out orders, and they didn't include killing the guy. If we had of done, the boss man would have surely done for us. No, you're wrong Berni, we did right. This way, having fed him and let him go, he may overlook the way you were heavy handed with him with your beatings. Anyway, we don't want no trouble, neither does the boss man. You better get on the blower (that's a phone in case you didn't know) and let him know we have carried out his orders to the letter. Then we may get paid and get out of this mess altogether."

Berni reached for the phone, as he did so, it rang before he could pick it up. The voice on the other end was clearly not happy. Berni grimaced and shuffled his feet, looking agitated and angry. "Yes boss, like you said boss, no boss, right away boss!" he passed the phone to Max.

"Yes boss, are you sure boss, sorry, no not questioning your decision boss, right away boss. We got it, orders is orders, what about our payment? No boss, of course not, need to do this job first, I understand boss. Right away boss. Goodbye."

"Now what? He changed his mind or something?"

"No Berni, but he's not happy. He wants us to get over to the island and sort out those two idiots who said to arrest the guy we just released. They've apparently screwed up."

"Why, what they done then?"

"I dunno, he didn't say, we'll get the rest of our orders when we get there and if we don't carry them out to the letter, he won't pay us."

"How we supposed to get there? Swim? It's miles and the ferries won't be running at this time of night."

"He said to take a dinghy or boat."

"What if we can't find one? Then I reckon we would have to swim."

Berni expressed his disagreement using a number of swearing words that made even Max's hair stand on end. After which, he grabbed hold of Max, "Come on then, the sooner we get this over and done, we can get some sleep and our money."

Stumbling to the door dragging Max with him, he swung it open and they both pushed their way out. The night air was hitting them full force from the tropical storm brewing, coming from the islands.

"Bl---y orders, I'm sick of em."

"Quit moaning, at least that guy didn't hold a grudge because we was only following orders, eh?"

Little did they know that guy Arthur, might not hold a grudge, but that may not reflect what his friends and family may think or do when the others were made aware of the whole episode that Arthur had endured.

So, both oblivious to what had occurred after his return to the hotel, and the possible outcomes, Max and Berni went off to find a boat to fulfil their orders.

Jean is reunited with Arthur:

Meanwhile back at the hotel, Arthur was snoring loudly in the chair, when his wife walked in. The night porter had advised her of the room service he had just provided to her husband.

Somewhat surprised to hear this, she hurriedly left the coffee lounges and returned to her room. Having left a message with the porter to inform the others, on their return, of her room number, should they wish to impart any updated information to her from their evening's efforts.

Jean quietly opened the door and stepped inside the room, she stood still just inside for a moment, to take in the scene. Arthur was asleep, in what looked a very uncomfortable position in the chair. He was wearing a tracksuit, as if preparing to go jogging. His face was puffy and bruised in places, loud snoring noises were coming from his nose and mouth.

Jean gasped at the sight of him. Instinctively running across to him, to hug him and wake him up, she stopped short, for fear of his reaction if awoken suddenly. After all, he had clearly been in some sort of accident or fight.

Instead, she decided to pour two coffees and a brandy for herself, then gently whilst speaking softly, shook him until he was awake.

16: THE CHILDREN AND MOMBO

Inside Mombos' house

As mentioned, Daniel was unaware of what had been occurring at the hotel and within his parents' room.

He was instead sitting with the others in Mombo's place, having just eaten jerk chicken that his wife had made them all. He was struggling to focus on the conversation, as he kept drifting off into a daydream in which his father was telling him not to trust anyone. Only a few words seemed to penetrate his ears from the groups' conversation.

He was briefly aware of Mombo's wife asking about his stick, and commenting on its size and shape, also how he had come to have it.

Axel had immediately butted in and said that it was his, he had brought it with him, and quickly reminded the group that he had used it to catch and cook the fish that they had eaten earlier that night.

Not fully aware of what was happening, Daniel felt the atmosphere in the room change. Summer and Roman both caught on quickly and agreed that it was Axel's and that he must have left it behind at the bonfire when he left, and they had found it again whilst retracing their steps after Daniel was injured.

Noting Daniel's vague recognition and his drowsiness, Mombo suggested that they turn in for the night and get some sleep. The others agreed, then made attempts to move away from the table. Axel leant down and picked up the staff to give to Daniel. Straight away he felt a connection to it that gave him a feeling of strength through his body. He passed it to Daniel and as he did so the strength from the staff seemed to sear through them both, joining their minds as one.

The sense of imminent danger enveloped them both, they looked at each other and then the other two. Roman and Summer looked very drowsy, as if about to fall asleep. Roman went to stand up, but his legs gave out under him, Summer tried to catch at his arm to stop him but was unable to. Her strength was draining from her in front of their eyes.

Mombo and his wife took charge, they quickly lifted the two children up and carried them over to a large bed like structure. It looked as if they had made it from tree trunks, roughly cut to size with webbing from strips of oiled cotton and covered it with a mattress stuffed with straw.

It stretched 6 or 7 feet across the width of the room. Even though roughly hewn, it was strong and easily took their weight.

Axel and Daniel watched them, unsure if they intended harm or just kindness and care. They felt as if they were all locked in a bubble suspended in time, too scared to breathe in case the bubble broke and danger took over.

After a few seconds which seemed like hours, Mombo turned to them, "Come you two, you must be very tired too. There is enough room for the four of you on here. It's late, you need to rest and sleep for a while if you are to be ready to take a boat back to the mainland tomorrow."

Axel and Daniel somehow knew that they had to get over too Roman and Summer, to help them. They joined hands, and with Daniel leaning heavily on the staff, walked the short distance to the bed and sat with the others. Keeping hold of the staff, they reached out and held hands with Summer and Roman. An immediate sense of strength filtered through the children.

Mombo brought blankets over to them and covered them. Soon, they had regained some of their bodily strength, their tiredness took over and they drifted off to sleep.

Roman and Summer slept soundly, Daniel was very restless, with dreams of his father mixed with those of the old man with dangerous figures, their faces blurred, drifting in and out.

Axel was the last to fall asleep, he was a light sleeper and easily disturbed. He had been listening to the conversation between Mombo and his wife. He was doing his best to remain alert. He eventually drifted into sleep but not before he had heard them say that they needed to get the children off the island as they were in danger; that whilst they remained there, it meant none of them were safe, including Jethro.

Axel was surprised to hear Jethro's name. Did Mombo know him? Were they in league together? Did this mean that they couldn't trust any of them? Unable to settle properly, he drifted in and out of sleep. Every now and again, hearing snippets of conversation.

"We will have to smuggle them out with the old man and girl, unless we can get them onto the next ferry." He heard them say.

"The storm is abating, the ferry should run, we need to get a message through to Jethro."

He dozed some more, then woke again to the sound of the door slamming as a draft caught it from the storm outside. Feeling sleepy and muddled in his head, he turned toward the door, just as Mombo slipped out.

Mombo leaves the house and seeks help:

Feeling chilled from the draft, he pulled the blanket round himself and moved closer to Daniel and the staff. He wanted to wake Daniel, and tell him what was occurring, he was concerned however, that Mombo's wife would hear and cause trouble. He gave Daniel a little shake, then whispered into his ear as carefully and quietly as he could.

"Shush you two, you will wake the others. Go to sleep now, you need to rest ready for tomorrow. Rest now, you are quite safe, all will be clear in the morning." Then Mombo's wife pulled the blankets further over them and said a few unintelligible words. Within minutes, both boys were asleep.

Mombo in the meantime, was scouring the island whilst being lashed by wind and rain. He needed to find Jethro and the ferry man before morning. He knew that he needed to do so before the rain worsened.

Jethro in the meantime, was oblivious to Mombo's concerns. He was asleep in his bed dreaming of seeing Summer again. Even though she was very young, he found her appealing, feisty, tomboyish, yet naive. He liked girls like that. He could have fun with them, showing them around, spending time with them. It made him feel young and carefree, not shackled to a job that he hated and only paid peanuts.

Having this week off had been beneficial to him, his plans were unfolding nicely. He had formulated them long before he had met the children, having overheard conversations at the airport. He had known there was more to these families than they had realised. He knew that if he stayed close to their trail, he would come off well in the end. He could use his contacts to arrange whatever he needed. He had no ties and could come and go as he pleased. His holiday had come at a good time, and he was going to make the most of it. He was feeling invincible and would not stop until he had achieved his aim.

Had Jethro been aware of Mombo's angry thoughts, he may have been more hesitant in his planning. This, however, was not the case, and he slept oblivious of any concern of Mombo wanting to change his plan. Unaware that whilst he was laying there, enjoying his dreams, Mombo had left his home and his wife to care for the children, whilst he had come to look for him.

Mombo had first tried the guest hut that he knew Jethro rented when he visited the island. He had not found him there, so had looked in the bars and night clubs for him. A common place for him to be found. This was also unsuccessful, as he found them to be closed up, with palm shutters barricaded against doorways to protect them from the wind and rain. Racking his brains to see if he could dredge up a memory of somewhere else he had seen him before, to know where he would be. Mombo stood in the pouring rain, feeling angry and frustrated. Wet and chilled from the wind, he tried to think like Jethro. Where would he go? What things did he enjoy doing? It then struck him that he should try the caves. He would shelter there himself and probably find Jethro doing the same. Jethro, after all, used them to hoard his ill-gotten gains. He was clever like that. He portrayed himself as a pleasant helpful young man, yet all the time he was plotting some sinister plan.

Having first met the lad when he, Mombo, had returned to the island on completion of his last medical training, he had thought him to be a happy go lucky holiday maker who had latched onto his wife for companionship, in a strange new holiday environment. It was only as he had got to know him over the subsequent years, he had realised that there was a much darker part to Jethro that he didn't like or trust.

Mombo soon arrived at the caves. He entered the first one which was empty, no sign of any use recently. The next ones he found, turned out to be those where Summer had been held. He was unaware of this at the time. He was surprised to see makeshift bedding and stuff laying around that suggested it had been used recently. He thought maybe Jethro had been using it. There was, however, no sign of Jethro or any of his friends there.

Mombo tried the next few caves without success and was just giving up when he came across another one hidden well behind a rock. He ventured inside, looking around, he noticed footprints leading into the back of the cave which is where he found Jethro sound asleep. He shook him awake much to Jethro's annoyance.

“What the heck, what you doing here? Leave me alone, I need my sleep.”

“I'm not going anywhere until I've said what I came to say.”

“Well, be quick about it, then get out!”

“You've gone too far this time Jethro, too far I say!”

“What are you talking about?”

“You have put those children in danger from your strange friends. You do realise they have been drugging the young girl, to get information out of her? Why you can't just get your artefacts the legal way like everyone else, I don't know. You created this mess, and you need to get it sorted, before these kids get badly harmed. We need to get them back to the mainland safely in the morning, before the police come looking for them. Can your ferry man be trusted?”

“Hold on there, you are making a big mistake. I didn't arrange for anyone to be drugged or kidnapped or anything else.”

“Well, if you didn't, I don't know who did, which makes things much worse. So, answer me. Is your boatman trustworthy? Or was he in on the kids being treated like prisoners on the island?”

"I have no idea what you're talking about, they were safe when I left them and looking to secure a boat trip back to the mainland. I've never had any problems with the guy. I admit he's old and a bit forgetful, but pretty safe I would have thought. Is that where they are, has he agreed to take them across?"

"No, that is, they were there, but they're not now. He had agreed to take them across in the morning, but he seems to have disappeared and the kids have had a rough time of it.

"Are they safe now?"

"Yes, but I don't know how long for, so we need to move fast. Can you track down your boatman, and bring him to my place? My wife will fix you something to eat whilst we make plans to get them out safely and back to the mainland. Can I trust you to do that?"

"Sure, you can. I admit I wanted to follow them to find out what they knew, but I didn't wish them any harm."

"We better get going then."

Jethro grabbed his jacket, torch, pocket- knife and watch, before leaving the cave together, then separating to go their different ways.

Mombo was still unsure if he could fully trust Jethro but told himself that he had no other choice. Hoping that Jethro had a few morals and a shred of real kindness in him.

Mombo returned to his home. His wife was pleased to see him, he confirmed that he had found Jethro, that all was good.

He noticed that she was cutting up herbs, which although not unusual for her, it surprised Mombo to see her doing it at this time of night. He recalled seeing her doing it earlier as well, when preparing the dinner,

It struck him that maybe his wife had deliberately drugged the children, to make sure that they did not run away. Even though he could see why she may have done this, he did not approve. He found himself worrying about whether he could trust her, any more than Jethro.

Jethro, however, was proving to be reliable at least. He had tracked down his ferry man.

He, like Jethro, was not happy to be awakened from his sleep. The banging on his door made him fear for his life. Only when he realised it was Jethro, did his heart stop beating so fast. He had lumbered over to his door to open it, but not before checking through his window to see who or what was out there.

"What do you want, can't a man sleep without being disturbed?"

"Did you or did you not agree to take four children over to the mainland in the morning?"

"What's it to you if I did or not?"

"Just answer the question, old man, and be quick about it."

"If you mean the kids I let sleep in the boathouse, then yer I did. Why? Do you have a problem with that?"

"Yes, I mean them. Did you arrange for one of them to be kidnapped or locked in?"

"No! Course I didn't. What do you take me for? I may be a smuggler, but I haven't stooped to harming children!"

"Then we need to hurry and get back to them and smuggle them onto your ferry to get them to the mainland in the morning, before whoever is after them finds them again."

"Where are they now?"

"At Dr Mombo's place and may be in danger, they're pretty-well exhausted. The doctor and his wife are with them."

"Who are they?"

"Never mind, are you going to help us or not?"

"Ok give us a few minutes to get dressed, but I'll need payment!"

"Don't worry you'll get your money."

The boatman quickly dressed and joined Jethro.

"Lead the way, but this better not be a wild goose chase. I don't like being disturbed at night for some joke."

"Don't worry old man, it's not. I said you're reliable and can be trusted, so I hope I'm right, these kids have been through quite an ordeal and need our help."

Mombo succeeds in getting help:

Having confirmed his support, the two men made their way to the doctor's hut.

The doctor and his wife were sitting waiting for them, the kids appeared to be asleep. There was an atmosphere in the hut that suggested the two adults had argued about something.

"Come in you two, my wife will cook you some jerk chicken whilst we make a plan. I do not think we can just let the children walk onto the ferry in the morning, as they could be seen and in danger. Someone must be trying to prevent them from doing something, or why would they have abducted Summer?"

The two men entered the hut, and Mombo's wife set to making food for them. Mombo kept an eye on her to ensure she did not put any herbs in that could drug them. He still did not trust her and thought she may be in league with Jethro.

They decided that the best plan would be to smuggle them out by boat, failing that, they should sneak them onto the ferry that night. Once they reached the quay on the Miami side, they may be safer and able to make their way back to their hotel.

If need be, Mombo could travel with them and explain that they missed their ferry, as Summer was unwell and needed treatment and rest.

With this latter plan in mind, they sent the ferry man off to make ready a safe place to stow the children on his ferry. They could not risk using the boathouse, so they would have to smuggle them direct to the ferry. Mombo decided that they should use his ambulance, and so the children would be lifted into it. Axel still clung to Daniel's hand and the stick, although still drowsy, he was sufficiently awake to take in what was happening. Mombo explained their plan to him and told him to relax, all would be fine.

17: BACK ON THE MAINLAND THE SAGA CONTINUES

Back at the hotel, Jean was hearing from Arthur about his ordeal. After her initial shock of finding him in the hotel room, being horrified at the sight of his injuries, she rang reception and asked them to send up some first aid supplies, fresh coffee and biscuits.

Then she informed them that Arthur was no longer missing. Jean also asked them to inform the local police of his return.

After Jean had helped Arthur to bed properly and tended to his bruises, she went along to Axel's parents and informed them that he had returned. Then contacted the other parents, before retiring for the night.

There had been no news regarding the children's whereabouts, therefore the parents had concluded that due to the late hour, it was unlikely that they would return before the morning.

With no news either, about the professor from the police, they presumed that they'd made no headway in finding him or the children. In view of the lack of help and support provided by the police, they were reluctant to raise too much fuss, for fear that the hotel would ask them to leave. They were unaware of whom to trust as the two officers that had allegedly arrested Arthur, had been fakes. They also appeared to be in league with someone in the police, high up.

Some of the parents however were still anxious about finding the children and couldn't be mollified. Jean also wondered about the old man, had he fallen foul of the police, or was it a form of conspiracy? Why would a taxi driver not take him to the right hotel? After all, they gave him clear instructions. What was so special about him, that two people masqueraded as detectives, just to pump Arthur for information about him? None of it made sense, yet she was determined to get to the bottom of it.

Little did she know, that the said masquerading officers were now on their way over to the islands, still following orders.

18: THE VILLAINS HAVE ORDERS FROM THE BOSS

"Boss man says the guys have messed up bad. They gave him wrong information about that guy we picked up. They also captured one of the kids and drugged her. Then the idiots let her escape, so now she is loose on the island. We are supposed to pick up the professor guy and some woman. They however got the wrong female. The boss is fuming. He reckons we can find them and waste them, before someone else finds them and drags the truth out of them."

"That's all very well but we don't know where they live, do we, and it's a foul night, they could be anywhere."

"Orders is orders. We've got to get over to the island, then ring the boss when we arrive, then the boss will tell us were to go to find them."

"What if we get stopped, the place could be crawling with police, after all they could be out looking for that girl you said had escaped."

"We will just have to be careful and if anyone says anything, we'll have to plead ignorance. That shouldn't be difficult for you, should it?"

Max and Berni made their way to Miami harbour whilst engaged in their conversation and were soon sniffing out a dinghy to row across to the islands, luckily for them however, Max spotted a motorboat and with a little bit of manoeuvring, was able to get it started and swing it out from the quay into the open sea.

Max had been a seasoned sailor, having spent a number of years in the navy before retiring. It was then he had fallen on hard times and had fallen foul of the police.

Desperate for money, he had got involved in crime. He was eventually, recruited as an odd job man by the boss. Most jobs involved stealing or fencing stolen goods, but some involved violence.

He had been teamed up with the tall guy, as they made a good team for entering places to burgle. He didn't much like his partner though, as he was unpredictable and needed keeping in line.

Even though, much smaller than him, Max was able to keep him under control. He had years of knocking new sailor recruits into line. This was no different they just had to follow orders.

A couple of hours went by, and the storm smashed the boat about on the normally calm sea, it was nearing dawn when they pulled into harbour.

"Land at last, now what we supposed to do?"

Max explained the rest of the boss's orders, "We got to go and get the two guys from their home, to get a description of the girl from them. We need to try and stop her from getting the ferry back to the mainland. She's one of a group of kids, so we got to watch for her at the ferry."

"How do we know which ferry to watch?"

"Well, I don't know, I hadn't thought of that! We'll have to split up and take a ferry each. They can't be that hard to spot, so as soon as one of us sees them, we can contact the other one. We will have to use the two guys the boss wants us to waste, they can help us identify the girl. We can always do away with them once we have the kid. The boss is going to meet us at the main quay when he knows we have got her. So soon as we get her, we contact him."

"That's enough talking, we need to get going if we are going to find them before dawn."

The two men dragged the boat to its mooring and secured the rope. They then set off together to find the two men. The boss had given them the rough addresses, so all they had to do was find them. It wasn't long before they were soaked through and feeling miserable. Eventually they found the house where the guys were staying. It was all in darkness, so they guessed they were probably sleeping.

After breaking their way in, they held them hostage until they agreed to identify the children and assist with preventing them from returning on the ferry. Max told them they would be, rewarded by the boss for their help.

The two guys, feeling stupid, stood there in their night wear with a gun pointing at them, they were in no doubt that the tall guy would shoot them if they didn't agree. That it was only because the little guy was keeping him in check, that he hadn't done so already.

"Ok, ok, we'll do what you asked, but let us get dressed first and eat."

"Sure, you can, but you try and trick us, he won't hesitate to waste you. Got it?"

"Yeah!"

The two men went and got dressed, then they all sat and ate some food that would hopefully sustain them for a good while, as none of them knew when they would get their next meal. They had orders to carry out and until they were completed to the boss's satisfaction, nothing else mattered. They were grateful for the food they had been given and made sure they had their fill.

Having discussed their plan over the meal, they finished and set off again into the foul weather, although it was not as bad as it had been, as the storm appeared to be abating.

19: THE VILLAIN'S PLAN AND MOMBO'S PLAN CONFLICT

Unknown to Mombo and Jethro, the guys from the mainland and villains that had drugged Summer, had teamed up together to watch the ferries and intercept Summer. Unknown to the villains, Mombo and Jethro were arranging with the ferry man to smuggle the children onto the ferry in the early morning. They were making plans about the children, with Mombo unaware, that they may be heading into a trap.

Mombo still wasn't very sure if he could trust the ferryman, or his own wife, come to that, he was keeping a close eye on them. Jethro, so far, had come through and appeared genuine in his concern for the children, particularly Summer, so he was satisfied that the plan they had made should work.

As soon as the time was right, they woke the children and fed them. Then, wrapping them in blankets, they put them in the truck Mombo used as an ambulance. The children were told to remain quiet and still. That they were to be taken to the ferry as agreed the night before with the ferry man. There, they would be put onto the ferry before all the other passengers arrived.

Daniel had listened to the plan and with his head a little clearer after his night's sleep, he realised that they had made arrangements with the ferry man to pay him

Thinking this could be a problem, he suddenly blurted out loud, "But what about the money, we don't have very much, is he still willing to take us if we can't pay him a full fare?"

"Don't worry about that Daniel, you can keep your money, we will sort that out. All you lot have to do is what we ask, then all will be well."

"Thank you, sir, we will."

Mombo and Jethro got into the truck, Mombo in the driver seat, Jethro in the back with the children. They had arranged for his wife to remain at their home, in case anyone came looking for them, or needed the doctor's help.

This way she could explain that he was out on a call but would contact them on his return. That way no awkward questions should arise.

The plan was to meet the ferry man at his ferry in the hope that he had made ready, a good place to stow the children. Mombo had told his wife this much, but not which ferry service, in case she was untrustworthy.

They took off in the truck, the night storm was calming, the sky was no longer pitch black. The sun would be rising soon, and the full extent of the storm's devastation would be visible.

Even though the islanders were used to these storms, they dreaded them coming, as much clearing up was needed, and many people needing help and support.

It was fortunate for Mombo and the children that the storm was relenting, as this would mean that the ferries would be able to run.

It wasn't long before the truck pulled up at the quay. Mombo flashed his headlights twice to let the ferryman know they had arrived.

He got no response, so he flashed them twice again.

There was still no, response, everything was quiet, as if the quay and the ferry were deserted.

"Hey Jethro, you sure your guy's reliable, he doesn't appear to be here as arranged?"

"He's never let me down before."

"In that case, I'll go and explore and see if he has been and gone home again."

"No Mombo, you stay here, if he doesn't turn up in ten minutes, I'll go and look. I know my way around the ferry, and if necessary, you can move the truck if anyone comes."

Jethro climbed aboard the ferry. It was quite a large vessel with seats front and back. The ferry had seen better days, the floor creaked as he walked. The well-trodden boards were well worn and in need of care and attention. The benches were marked with penknife scoring that people had done to leave their name or number. The engine cabin had an aroma of male sweat, engine oil, and stale food.

The boat had an eerie stillness, as if it had been left to rot, forgotten about and unused for some time. It lay wedged against the dock side and reflected its owners age and infirmity. It was much smaller and older than the more modern ferries that ran from the various ports around the islands. It was generally used as a short shuttle ferry when the others were fully booked.

Jethro walked round the ferry looking for signs of the old ferryman but was unable to locate him.

He was perplexed, as he considered him to be reliable, and thought therefore maybe they needed to wait a while longer for him or check and see if he was at the boat shed.

Jethro turned to return to the truck and seek Mombo's view on this, but as he did so he glanced across the harbour, and noticed a small dinghy tied alongside. At first this did not seem at all strange, after all there was boats of all shapes and sizes around. It was the shape of something laying in the dinghy and the old coat that appeared to lay over it that caught his attention.

He climbed off the ferry and gingerly dropped himself into the small dinghy. On moving the coat, he realised that his concerns had been justified. There beneath the coat lay the ferry man, his head was cut and bleeding. He was alive but clearly needed help. Jethro quickly made the man comfortable and climbed back onto the ferry and made his way back to the truck.

Mombo was concerned on hearing Jethro' s news, and immediately agreed to help him lift the man off the dinghy, back on to the ferry and treat his wound.

The children were safely tucked up in the truck, and after

dressing his wound the ferry man was also put in there.

Having told Mombo and Jethro that he was attacked by a man wanting to know where the children were, they all realised the ferries were being watched and therefore not safe to transport them to the mainland.

"Now what do we do? We can't just dump the kids"

"No Jethro, we can't, I have only one alternative, but it will be tricky. I will stow the children away somewhere safe. I don't think the felons will bother with watching this ferry now, after attacking the boatman. Then if you are both agreeable, I will meet you at the main ferry, on which the children would have returned. The felons are likely to be watching to see if they get on the boat."

"Why yes of course, so we will be able to identify them, then prevent them harming the children".

Mombo drove the truck away from the quay, then, turned in the direction of the other port. He drove through the, storm, ravaged countryside for a while until he reached a clearing not far from the port.

The children were awake now, so Mombo explained his plan.

He found it was going to be trickier than he first thought, as the children were insisting they get on the ferry and draw the villains out.

He insisted, however, that they be stowed away on his boat, for safety.

In the end, they agreed to allow Axel and Summer to come on

to the ferry quay, whilst the other two waited on Mombo's boat.

Mombo dropped off Jethro and the boatman, agreeing to return with Summer and Axel as soon as he had stowed the other two away. He did not wish to identify his boat to Jethro or the boatman, in case they were not fully trustworthy.

They then drove round the harbour to the quay where the smaller boats were moored.

"Ok you two, out you come. You will be quite safe here if you stay down below and out of sight. I have a couple of friends down there, who are also hiding out so try not to disturb them too much. We will get you all to the mainland as soon as it is safe to do so."

Roman helped steady Daniel and gave him his stick, as Mombo lifted him off the back of the truck and put him upright on the ground.

"Are you sure you wouldn't want Axel to stay behind, after all I was with Summer when we got off the jetty, and surely they would expect me to be with her getting back on, not Axel?"

"You could be right there Roman, maybe we should tell Dr Mombo, I'm sure Axel wouldn't mind changing."

Once steadied on his feet, Daniel, turned to Dr Mombo,

"Thank you, doctor, but Roman has just pointed out that he got off the jetty with Summer. The villains are likely to expect him to be with her when she gets back on the ferry. It might therefore be better if Axel stays with me and you take Roman instead."

"Ok, if you think that's best, Roman can you quickly change places with Axel, as we have been here too long already and need to get back to the others."

The two boys did as they were bid. After which, Mombo instructed Axel and Daniel to board his boat.

They were both stiff from being cooped up in the truck, however they both managed to haul themselves over the side of the boat and disappear down into the berth below. Mombo's words still, ringing in their ears, to stay quiet and hidden until his return.

Mombo quickly turned the truck round and sped off to the ferry port with the other two on board.

"Hold on to me Summer, if the truck gets too bouncy."

"Thanks, Roman, Mombo seems to be in a hurry. I thought I was going to be sick as he swerved the truck round and over the bumps."

"Don't worry, it's probably just the sudden movement that's made your tummy feel funny, a bit like when you're on a roller coaster."

"Yes, you're right Roman, that's just how it was but without the fun."

They both laughed.

"Go back to sleep, you two. I'll wake you when we get there, rest as much as you can as you have a long day ahead of you."

It wasn't many miles to the port, but Mombo knew the children had been through a lot already, especially Summer. Even so, he was pleased to hear their laughter, as it meant that at last, they were able to release some of their tension and fear from their ordeals.

He was hopeful that they would track down the kidnappers, but first he had to meet up with and brief Jethro and Tom, the ferry man.

Unsure if the kidnappers were planning to intercept the children, but aware that they may do given the attack on Tom, Mombo didn't want to take any unnecessary chances of the children being seen before the ferry was due to be boarded.

Mombo pulled up at a quiet track not far from the ferry port. He took out a pair of binoculars and used them to survey the surrounding area. There was no sign of any parked cars or other forms of transport nearby. It was early, the normal hustle and bustle of the port was yet to start. He drove the truck closer to the port entrance, keeping close to the palm trees that lined the side of the track. He stopped a few yards from the entrance to the port and with his binoculars checked the area again.

He was reasonably satisfied that there was no one hiding there. He parked up and settled back to wait for the port to come alive. He didn't have to wait long, as the weather warmed up. Apart from the obvious devastation caused by the wind and rain on the buildings and trees, all signs of the storm disappeared. Movement could be seen rapidly increasing across the port. Trucks started arriving with their produce and wares.

Boat crews and fishermen appeared out of the shadows. People carrying cases and various offspring, started to arrive and queue at the side of the ferry office. The noise level increased with the chatter and shouting, mixed with music that sang from their radios and voices.

Mombo peered through his binoculars, trying to identify Jethro and Tom. He needed to talk them through his plan for getting the children on board unharmed. He realised that this would mean drawing the villains out and could put the children at risk. He needed Jethro and Tom to keep lookout and intervene if they saw any attempts against the children. Another ten minutes passed before he spotted them, they were leaning up against the railing of the ferry gangplank.

Locking the children in the truck, Mombo made his way across to them. Whilst he did so, he scoured the area for people that looked out of place. It was impossible to be sure about some of the people in the crowds, but the ones he didn't like the look of, he would point out to Jethro.

"Good morning, I'm glad to see you made it, I've spotted a few unsavoury looking guys who may be the felons that are after the children, they are just over there by the jetty. I reckon it will be busy today, with people wanting to get back to the mainland after that storm. I see the press are here already."

"Yeah, they've just arrived. They're probably doing a piece on visitors fleeing the island, following the aftermath of the storm. So long as they don't get in our way, they're fine."

"What's the plan then? Me and Jethro 'ave been, hanging around here for some time now, it's getting a bit conspicuous, like."

"Where are the kids?"

"They're safe, I've two in the van and two hidden away, I

reckon if I take the two aboard, the guys who abducted them before, might try again. I need you two to keep an eye out and intervene. If we can get these two stashed on board, I'll go and get the other two and do the same with them."

20: AXEL & DANIEL ALSO HAVE A PLAN

Little did Mombo know, his plan was being scuppered before it had started. Back at his boat, Daniel and Axel were not happy about the situation.

Having reached the berth below in the boat, which opened out into a large living space that appeared to house a cooking area, dining section and separate sleeping quarters, the two boys felt an immediate sense of unease.

“Daniel, are you alright?” whispered Axel, “it's a bit dark and eerie in here.”

“Yes Axel, I feel it too,” he whispered back, “I can't see much, just the outline of the room.”

“Mombo said that he had two others stashed away down here, I don't want to trip over them.”

“Let's sit on this bench a while and gather our thoughts.”

The two boys sat on the bench which separated the galley kitchen from the dining area. In doing so, Daniel let go of his stick and it dropped to the floor. The noise seemed shattering, in the creepy stillness of the darkness.

Axel bent down to pick it up and noticed a slight glow coming from it. At first, he thought he imagined it, but when he looked again, it was still there.

"Daniel, look at your stick, it's by your feet."

"Oh! don't worry, Axel, it can stay there for a while, I don't need it whilst I'm sitting down."

"No Daniel, you don't understand, look!" Axel's voice grew louder with a sound of urgency in it.

"Shh, Axel, we are supposed to be quiet, I tell you I don't need it at the moment, if you're so worried about it, pick it up yourself."

Axel grabbed Daniel's arm and tried to bend him to pick his stick up. "Ouch stop that, what's come over you? I tell you; I don't need it just now."

Exasperated by Daniel's stubbornness, Axel bent down and picked up the stick. As he did so, the glowing receded and it looked its old, crooked self again.

Axel sat back on the bench, feeling tired and strange. He was wondering if the weird atmosphere was playing tricks on his mind. He was sure he had seen the glow on the stick. He questioned whether it had just been a trick of the light, perhaps a glimmer of light from the moon, shining through the porthole, or a flash of lightning.

He was cursing Daniel for not looking, when he suddenly realised that he hadn't told Daniel what he had seen at the newspaper office or about the significance of the stick he was using.

Though they had all gone along with his story that he had

brought the stick with him, and then dropped it on the sand where they cooked the fish. None of them knew why he had laid claim to it. Axel started to feel rather sheepish. He was angry with Daniel for no reason, as Daniel was unaware of the significance of the stick.

He turned to Daniel, about to say something when he stopped himself, remembering that they were not alone in the boat.

"What's up Axel? You seem very odd, didn't you get much sleep or you afraid of the dark?"

"No! I'm not, it's just something don't feel right and I'm worried about Summer and Roman."

"Yes! you're right," Daniel whispered. "I feel it too, we are here stuck on this boat, whilst they may be heading into danger."

"Yes! and we may be in danger here too. Mombo said he had other people hiding out on this boat. We don't know who they are, they could be the guys that kidnapped Summer or locked Roman in the boat shed."

"Yes, I agree Axel, but what can we do about it? I admit I sense danger here and, in my head, my father's voice keeps warning me to trust no-one."

"We can't just sit here, there's nothing for it, they can't come to us, so we'll just have to sail the boat to them."

"Wow, what a smashing idea, but stupid! How are we going to do that? Seeing as we have never sailed it before."

"Maybe not, but it can't be too hard. You can steer it, so you won't have to hobble about but just lean on your stick. Then, once we've set the course, I'll navigate. It will be an adventure."

"Yes, it will certainly be an adventure! But what about the other people on board, what do we do with them?"

"Oh, hang them, they can just stay hidden, we won't disturb them."

"Well, I hope you're right!"

"Ok let's do it."

Grinning at each other, they allowed their excitement and sense of adventure to take over and quash their fears.

The boys scrambled out of the berth below deck, onto the deck above. With Axel's help, Daniel hobbled over to the engine room and steering wheel. He leaned heavily on the stick with one hand whilst holding the wheel with the other one. Axel studied the charts and instruments, denoting the direction.

"Ready, Daniel?"

"Yes, ready, start the engine."

The engine started, and the boat lurched forward but didn't move any further.

"Hey Axel, you need to untie the boat from the mooring post so we can move away, oh and you better do it quick, before someone tries to stop us."

Whilst the engine was still running, Axel hastily jumped off the boat and untied the mooring, throwing the rope back aboard as he jumped back on.

"Off we go then Daniel, all aboard."

Daniel steered the boat out of the mooring successfully this time and they moved further and further away, gradually increasing speed as they did so.

"This is fun, what an adventure!"

They hadn't been going for long when they heard noises from below. Someone was moving about.

"Oh, Daniel, our passengers are on the move, we better put a spurt on, in case they try and stop us."

As he increased the speed Daniel swung the boat round toward the direction of the ferry quay.

The boys heard muffled voices, as they sailed, coming from below, then a noise on the stairs of footsteps. Expecting to be jumped on by cutthroats and villains, they took out their meagre weapons. The footsteps became louder, as they got, closer, the boys tried not to make a noise and held their breath. A covered head appeared out of the top of the stairway, as it did so, the boys stared in amazement. As the cover fell from the head, they saw much to their disbelief, a woman. It was not, however, just any woman, but the lady that they had spoken to at the newspaper office.

In unison the boys gasped, "It's you! What are you doing here?"

"I was about to ask you the same thing," replied the lady. "What are you doing on board this boat and where are you taking it to?"

Daniel found his voice first. "We are taking it to the main ferry port, to rescue our friends. If you try to stop us, we will kill you." The boys pulled out their weapons, Axel his knife, Daniel his gun. They didn't mean it, but they hoped the lady would believe them and let them be.

Instead, she laughed, "How did you get on this boat? Who brought you here?"

"What's it to you? Who brought you, here?"

"Oh, that's easy, my friend owns this boat."

"Well so does ours."

She laughed again, seemingly unperturbed by their weapons and manner.

"Tell me what makes you think your friends are in danger?"

Daniel, who was struggling to stand and steer the boat at the same time, dropped his guard. "If you must know, someone we don't know, kidnapped our friend Summer and drugged her before. We think they may try again. So, we need to get there fast in case they do."

"Someone also locked our friend Roman in the boat shed, and we don't know who that was either, do we Axel?"

This time the lady didn't laugh, she became very still, her face took on an angry look making the boys feel very uneasy. Could they have made a mistake trusting her with their information. It was as if they were all suspended in time for a few minutes, in a bubble, unable to make a sound. The bubble then burst as she exploded.

"How dare they do that to innocent children and why?"

"They think we know where the old man's gone, but we don't."

"What old man?"

Whilst Axel took over the steering of the boat, Daniel regaled the lady with their story.

"You know, the old man that we came to the newspaper about earlier when we met you. We were looking for him as he had asked for our help. My Dad and I had gone to see him at his hotel, he wasn't there. We are still trying to find him. We think someone is trying to prevent us. Your colleague said that whoever put the advertisement in the paper wasn't known to him. The reporter that had been asked to print it was away and not available. We don't know, but we think the newspaper article that is advertising a reward for information on the whereabouts of a missing professor, may be about the same man that we are looking for. We are not after the, reward we are just worried about him, as he seemed so upset and confused. My mother had arranged for him to be taken to the Miami Beach Hotel by taxi after he arrived at the Miami Hotel, thinking he was booked in there. On listening to the argument between him and the receptionist she realised his mistake."

"Of course! Now I remember, I'm sorry but I didn't recognise you. How come you two be on this boat? You said it belonged to a friend. Surely you don't have any from the island, if you have only just arrived on holiday? Who is your friend?"

Unsure if he had said too much, Daniel tried to avoid giving out Mombo's name.

"Oh! But you must know, for you said this boat belongs to your friend also."

His answer was met with a look of, surprise, which changed to a tight-lipped smile.

"Ah, so you don't trust me, well if you wish to continue sailing this boat, I suggest you do."

Even less, sure, how to respond Daniel looked away to Axel for some help. As he did so, the boat lurched suddenly as it leered on the turn, throwing Daniel off balance. He fell in a heap at the top of the stairs that led to the berth below. The sound of his voice in a shriek of, pain pierced though their ears. This was followed by a clatter of shoe heels and bones from the lady slipping on the metal stairs, and a scream, almost as painful as Daniel's.

Axel, struggling to steady the boat, hampered by the waves from the swell of the water, clung to the steering wheel, powerless, to help his friend and the lady, in their plight.

Time seemed to stand still as the incident happened. The boat was eventually brought under control, only minutes having passed, yet all previous conversation having ceased.

Daniel dragged himself up, to a kneeling position, and called down the stair well to the lady.

"Are you ok? Can we help you?"

"I think you have done enough damage already! As soon as we reach dry land, I shall deal with you and your friend. In the meantime, I don't wish to hear another word from either of you. Do you understand?"

"We are really sorry, but Axel did his best to hold the boat when the wave hit."

"Well, if you are sorry now so be it, however, if your current arrogance and attitude continues, you will be even sorrier later."

The sound of retreating footsteps could then be heard on the passageway below.

Axel and Daniel exchanged glances. They simultaneously shrugged their shoulders, baffled by the attitude and behaviour of the lady. One minute she seemed very nice, but this soon changed to anger or frustration.

"Are you alright Daniel? You screamed so loud, it was deafening, did you hurt yourself badly?"

"I think so, it was mainly the shock and the pain that shot through my leg as I fell."

"I hope the lady isn't badly injured, we'll be in real trouble if she is, still it couldn't be helped, after all you didn't do it deliberately did you?"

"No Daniel, of course not!" But the look of innocence on his face soon changed to a smirk.

"Oh Axel, please say you didn't do it on purpose?"

"No of course not, you saw the wave didn't you, but you've got to admit it was pretty good timing."

With that, both boys fell about laughing.

"Careful Axel, or we will lose our hold on the steering wheel."

Realising that Daniel was right and that they were in a desperate hurry to find the others, Axel swiftly steadied the boat and headed toward the harbour.

They heard no more from the passengers hidden below, for which they were grateful. It wasn't too long before the harbour came in sight, and they slowed the engine to coast into it. They needed to navigate their way into the harbour carefully, without drawing attention to themselves.

Meanwhile on the quay side, the ferry port was bustling with activity. People were milling around, awaiting visitors to the island or awaiting the opportunity to use their ticket to board the ferry for their journey across to the mainland. Jethro and Tom the ferryman, were positioned near the main jetty. They were both doing their best to blend into the background, whilst avidly looking for anyone that may be attempting to abduct the children.

Mombo had wanted to inform the port authorities that an attempt to harm the children may occur. He was concerned that by doing so, he may accidently alert the would-be attackers. Not knowing who they were and if they had a man on the inside, he thought it best to say nothing and keep close vigil to ensure their safety.

The effects of the storm the previous night was being cleared up and the sun was high in the sky. The heat and humidity made Mombo sweat whilst he waited anxiously for the right moment to release the children and allow them to walk, unhindered, along the quayside to the ferry.

21: BACK AT THE HOTEL THE PARENTS HAVE A PLAN

Back at the hotel, Jean and Arthur were concerned about the children. Arthur was convinced that they had gone in search of the old man. They knew that Daniel had been upset and anxious when they had returned to the hotel, after not finding him resident at the Miami Beach Hotel.

Arthur had also been concerned as well as a little cross, having given up his time to take Daniel to see the man. They had not found him there, and more to the point, there was no record of him booking into the hotel.

He was convinced he had seen an advert in the Bahama newspaper, requesting information about the old man's whereabouts, also offering a reward. This, he told Jean, is what had attracted the children and led them to go off in such a hurry.

This was not the view of all the parents and a conflict arose between them. The other parents hadn't seen this advert. Instead, the one they had read, was about an adventure, with no mention of the old man. Instead, it was about exploring caves, island beaches and jungle. All of which they believed, had attracted the children's attention, and led them to get on a ferry to the islands.

Arthur expressed his concerns about the children, in view of his tiredness and recent ordeal, he reluctantly agreed that there was little he could do before the morning. Jean said he would be better getting some rest.

Jean was not convinced of Arthur's idea that the children had gone to seek out the old man. She did, however, think it very strange that, her husband had been abducted, by two bogus policemen. Jean acknowledged that there was a connection between Arthur's view, and the children's behaviour.

This set her thinking that the children may be in danger. Jean decided she must take control of the situation and arrange for some of them to catch the morning ferry to the island.

Since the children had left, they had all felt uneasy and experienced a sense of danger. Even though some of them had tried to ignore it or poo-poo it, it had worried them all, particularly when the children didn't return for their evening meal. After hatching a plan in her head, she slipped into bed and slept soundly until her alarm awoke her.

The phone rang loudly, Jean stretched out her arm to reach it, "Hello" she said in a sleepy voice, "Thank you."

Arthur stirred, "Who was that on the phone?"

"It was an early morning call, I forgot to say, I booked it last night."

Arthur groaned and turned over. There was a banging on the door and a muffled voice called "Room service!"

"Now what, doesn't anyone sleep in this hotel?"

"Sorry Arthur, but I ordered an early breakfast."

"What for?"

"Why, because I have a lot to organise if some of us are going to catch the ferry across to the island."

Arthur groaned again.

"Okay you get the door, whilst I get a quick shower."

Jean opened the door and the hotel porter wheeled in a trolley laden with hot coffee, croissants, boiled eggs and toast. She handed the porter a tip.

"Thank you, will that be all madam?"

"Yes, thank you, no wait, do you have a copy of the Ferry timetable for today?"

"I will fetch one immediately madam," and he turned and walked out of the room, returning a few minutes later with the timetable. Jean accepted it gratefully and gave him another tip then closed the door.

Suspecting that Arthur would be in the shower for a while, Jean did not wait for him before starting her breakfast. The coffee tasted good, she thought, with the croissants and helped her to focus on the day's tasks.

Meanwhile, Arthur was closeted in the shower room. He glanced at himself in the mirror then took a closer look. He wasn't a pretty sight. His face was blotchy and covered in bruises, his lip swollen, though not as bad as it had been the previous night. His limbs ached. He felt generally tired and stiff all over. After a grunt and few swear words, he ran the shower until it was hot and steamy, then ducked under it, revelling in the warmth on his tired bones. He washed himself all over both physically and mentally, trying to wash away the memory of his recent ordeal. After rubbing himself dry, he put on the large towelling bathrobe that hung on the door. Feeling a little refreshed, he joined Jean in the sitting room area of their suite and tucked into his breakfast.

Following a quick coffee together, Jean left Arthur to enjoy his food whilst she went to shower and dress. She also found the shower refreshing, removing some of her tiredness and helping her to think clearer. Having sent a message through to the others last night to say that Arthur had returned safely, albeit a bit worse for wear, Jean was hoping they would be willing to help her track down the children. Reluctant to take Arthur with her to the island, she had hoped to have some of the parents go with her instead. Arthur however was insistent. Jean had to acknowledge that, where Daniel was concerned, he was the best person to have along. Not because of his brawn or brains, but because they appeared to have some link between them that enabled them to know what the other one was thinking. She had noticed this often, but also recently when the two of them had met the old man. It was uncanny, as if he had completed a telepathic circle between them.

Laughing at herself and her silly thoughts, she hurried Arthur out of the room and down to the hotel foyer. Axel's father was there with Roman's, waiting to leave for the ferry. Summer's parents, Rebecca and Jed, had agreed to stay behind with Axel and Roman's mothers, Annalisa and Selina, in case the children turned up at the hotel.

Jean expressed her gratitude to them for their support.

The parents arrange to catch the ferry to Big Bahama Island:

"Okay Jean, the taxi is waiting outside, we have to go now if we are to catch the 7am ferry.

Jean took Arthur's arm and with Stefan and Tobias, they left the hotel and got into the waiting taxi.

"Where to lady?"

"Take us to the ferry boat quay for the Bahama Islands please and fast, we need to catch the 7 am ferry."

"Ok lady."

As soon as they were all seated, the taxi took off at speed. The driver ran through the gears, until he was at a smooth speed that enabled him to manoeuvre the car through the traffic. The road signs flashed in front of them or on the side of the road, as the car sped on. It wasn't long before the car screeched to a halt outside the ferry port.

"There you go lady, we're here, I hope that was quick enough for you."

Jean looked at the driver, who had turned to face her from the front seat. He sat there grinning at her, shocked face. Collecting her wits, she nodded at the driver and gave him a bundle of dollar bills.

They climbed out of the car and walked over to the quay side. The ferry was moored up at the edge by the jetty. The place was crawling with people. Many queuing to step aboard the ferry, many more queuing to buy last minute tickets. Billboards showed attractive pictures of what they could expect over on the islands. These depicted hot sandy beaches, tropical plants, marketplaces, tropical birds etc.

Jean looked at them briefly as she went past, her main thoughts were about getting to the island as soon as possible to find the children. Arthur on the other hand, was lost in thought about the potential danger. He was sure that the children had gone to find the old man and had run into trouble.

Feelings he had when he was abducted had come back into his head. The confusion and sense of danger to himself and the children, sending shivers down his spine.

He tried shrugging it off and realised that in time he may forget some of the pain and memories of it being inflicted on his person. It was still very raw in his memory and reinforced his feeling of danger and need to trust no-one.

Stefan was unsure what to think. On the one hand, they had thought the children had gone on an innocent, adventure, that held no real risks. Whereas on the other hand, with Arthur's insistence about the children's interest in finding the old man, coupled with his abduction and ill treatment, it was likely that they may have been harmed.

Tobias wasn't sure what the children had got themselves into. He was concerned for Axel as he didn't really know any of the children before breakfast the day before. He had encouraged Axel to go with Daniel, which had led to the four children going off together.

He was concerned for all the four children who had gone off on an adventure, which could have got them into serious trouble. After all, they had not returned for dinner as expected. Neither had they contacted them to let them know where they were, or what they were doing. He was surprised at this, as Axel was generally very good at keeping in touch. He hoped that it would all be sorted out soon, and they would find the children well and happy. He could see Jean was getting impatient standing queuing and knew that she was also very worried.

"Don't worry Jean, we will soon be on the ferry."

"I wish I was sure about that, Tobias, however this queue is endless." Jean stood in the queue to obtain tickets for the journey. The queue was moving very slowly. Jean was becoming very impatient. "Arthur, can you see what's holding this queue up? If we don't hurry, we will miss the ferry."

Arthur was talking to Stefan about the children, when he heard Jean call him with her request to investigate the time it was taking to get the tickets. Hearing the frustration in her voice, he turned to look at the length of the queue.

Seeing that Jean was right, that there was still a large number of people in front of them, he went to the front of the queue.

People, at first did their best to block him, but on seeing his bruised face they relented and let him by. On reaching the cubby hole where the ticket clerk sat, Arthur spoke to him quietly.

"My wife and I and our friends are concerned about the length of the queue and the long wait to buy tickets. We are anxious to get on this ferry to enable us to find our children who are missing and stranded on the island. The police have been informed of the situation and are helping to locate them. I would therefore be grateful if you could let me have four tickets now, so that we can board immediately. The police would no doubt reward you for your help and assistance toward us."

The ticket clerk stared at Arthur. He couldn't believe his ears. This man was, wanting to jump the queue and expected him to believe his story.

"I'm sorry mate, but I can't do that. I'd have everyone wanting to jump the queue with some sob story."

"It's no sob story, it's true, don't you read the papers or watch the news?"

"No mate I don't get time, see, my papers over there untouched 'cause the queue, as you pointed out, is too long."

Arthur felt for the guy but was determined to get the tickets.

"Look, why don't you look at it now, you'll see I'm telling the truth. It's on the front page."

"Why should I? What's in it for me?"

"Humour me, check it out and you could be in for a share of the reward."

"Now you are talking, You sure about that?"

An exasperated Arthur sighed and replied, "Yes, I'm sure, read your paper and see."

The ticket clerk turned and picked up his paper. Unfolding it, he turned to the front page. Sure enough, there was an article about the missing children and the old man and a reward.

"Okay, mate, four tickets you said, didn't you?"

"Yes, four adults please."

"Coming right up. You will make sure they know I helped you, won't you?"

"Yes, yes, please hurry and not a word to anyone about this, or the police investigation will be jeopardised."

The clerk handed over the tickets," I get it, hush hush, your secret's safe, I hope you find them."

"Thanks mate!" Arthur took the tickets and retreated to the back of the queue where Jean, Stefan and Tobias were still waiting.

"Right let's go," he said quietly holding up the tickets. "There's no time to lose."

Jean and Stefan both looked in amazement, then Jean kissed Arthur.

"Sorry you two, there's no time for that, let's go."

They both grinned at Stefan, then joined him and Tobias in a sprint to the ferry jetty. Once boarded, they found a seat on the inside and settled down and relaxed, in the knowledge that they would be at the island in a couple of hours which would enable them to look for the children. Not aware of the possible dangers that lay before them once they reached their destination.

22: ON BIG BAHAMA ISLAND

The children were unaware of their parents' plans, as much as the parents were, regarding those hatched by the children.

Axel slid the yacht into the quayside, without raising any concern. They dropped anchor and breathed a sigh of relief. "We've made it, and it looks like we're not too late!" The boys congratulated each other. "Well done, Axel!", "Well done, Daniel!"

"What now Daniel?"

"Well Axel, we need to find the others, but first I think we need to check if there's any food or drink down below for us to have."

"Good idea Daniel."

"We had better see if that lady, and her friend that is hiding with her, are ok. That was quite a fall she took, and she was very angry and upset. We don't want her to cause or get us into any trouble."

"They probably need to eat and drink also, that was quite a journey you navigated."

"The yacht went very well, but it wasn't the smoothest or shortest trip I've ever been on."

"Come on then, let's go and investigate the lower deck, who knows what or who we will find."

Axel went first. The darkness was intense compared to the sunlight they had basked in whilst on deck.

Feeling his way carefully down the ladder, he guided Daniel as best he could, down behind himself to prevent him falling. Daniel checked each of the steps below him with his stick, before treading on it. When they reached the bottom of the ladder like staircase, they felt their way along the cabin. Axel felt about for a light switch and finding one, he went to switch it on.

"Here it is Daniel," he whispered, "I'll switch it on then, we will soon be able to see everything".

"No Axel! Don't do that, we don't want to disturb the people hiding out. There must be some food and drink in these cupboards here. There's a small sink as well, so we can get some water. We can leave some out for them also, so that if they come out of hiding whilst we're looking for the others, they will be able to have some too. It doesn't seem so dark in here now that my eyes have adjusted to the change. There's the bench seat over there where we sat when we first arrived. We can sit there whilst we have anything we find, to drink or eat. Then make our way back up top."

"Okay Daniel, there's some biscuits and coke in this cupboard, it's not much, but it's better than nothing."

"There's some bananas here too, if we have one of these each with some biscuits and coke, we should be ok. We can leave the rest out on the side with some drinks for the others."

The boys helped themselves to the food and drink and made their way in the dark to the bench. As they sat down, Daniel dropped the stick onto the floor. Axel watched in amazement as it started to glow. Once again, he tried to get Daniel to look at it, but to no avail. He was more concerned with eating his banana and drinking his coke. He was however surprised, when he picked it up again, it sent a feeling of power and strength through his body.

Axel tried to explain about the staff and its secret, however Daniel was in no mood for listening. He was anxious to get started in finding the other children. He picked up his stick and adjusted his eyesight, then started to make his way up the ladderlike staircase.

"Hurry Axel, or we will waste too much time. We must try and find them, as I am sure they are in danger. We mustn't linger any longer."

"I'm coming, Daniel. Be careful or you will slip and hurt yourself. Let me help you."

"I'm okay, I can manage with my stick. It's getting late, please hurry."

"Don't worry, I'm right behind you."

The boys made their way up the stairs, to the deck above.

"Come on Axel, help me get over the side of the yacht. It will be nice to step onto dry land again."

"That's true, but it doesn't look very dry to me, it's been pouring of rain all night!"

"Very funny, ha ha!"

Axel helped Daniel step off the yacht. They walked to the

quayside where the ferries came and went from. The yacht rested quietly on its mooring. Axel had been careful in fitting it in amongst the others to prevent it from appearing conspicuous. Its hidden passengers waited for a while, before moving, anxious not to be recognised by anyone passing by or boarding the boat. The elderly gentleman lay stiff and drowsy under the bench. Mombo had taken the precaution in sedating him. He believed that this would reduce the level of stress to him, whilst stashed in his cramped hiding place.

The lady, however, was not sedated, but allowed to move around at will. This meant that she could care for the elderly man, as well as herself. Food and drinks were available to them, as well as more blankets and medication as needed.

The lady, having fallen down the steps, was feeling battered and bruised but kept this to herself rather than upset the elderly gentleman. She was curious as to how the two boys had been able to be on board. Could Mombo have arranged it. If so, why?

It had been a shock when the boy told her that they had been the ones that had visited the newspaper print works. The boys looked so dishevelled and worn out. The one who was injured appeared tense and unwell, unlike earlier when she had met them at the paper. What on earth could have happened to them to have changed them so much.

They mentioned that their friends were in danger, but she had not seen any friends there or previously when they came to the paper. It had only been the two of them. Then, they had been expressing concerns about the old man that was missing, but they did not mention him this time. It was all very strange. Aware that they had left the yacht, but also taken time to leave food and drink out for her and the elderly gentleman, she took the food and drink and made a mental note to thank them if she met them again. There was nothing she could do other than wait for Mombo to return, for to leave their hiding place would put them all in danger. She hoped that the wait wouldn't be too long.

Mombo meanwhile, was biding his time with the other two children. The ferry was due to run, however, it was to be delayed due to the storm damage and the clearance work that needed to be done before it could board passengers.

Warehouses along the quayside had suffered damage, trees had been uprooted and debris was floating in the water. The harbour had filled up with people and their wares, but many could not complete their transfer of goods until warehouses and equipment had been made safe. A group of harbour men and volunteers were busy tackling the clean-up required.

Mombo did not offer his services but sat with the children, watching from his truck nearby. He was conscious that time was passing. He had left the boys back at his yacht and they would be wondering why he was taking so long.

He was concerned that there was nothing he could do about it until he was sure that it was safe to get Summer and Roman aboard the ferry. Tom and Jethro were in place watching out for any one acting suspicious.

Summer and Roman were equally frustrated. They had been

cooped up in the truck for what seemed like hours to them. Even though it hadn't been that long, the waiting had seemed endless.

Their restlessness started to become more noticeable to Mombo, when they started questioning his plans.

"How much longer have we got to wait?"

"Why can't we get out now, after all, we can look after ourselves?"

"I'm sorry Summer, but I don't think you can, you know what has already happened to you and I don't want it to happen again. We need to get you back to your parents safely."

"Our parents will be worried about us, we need to get back to them as soon as possible, we can't just sit here."

"It won't be much longer, they have nearly finished the clearing up. Roman, make her understand. We need to be careful and try and catch who has been causing you harm, you must understand that"

"Summer, Mombo's right, we do need to be careful and patient or we will put Jethro at risk as well as ourselves."

"Yes! but how do we know Jethro is not in league with them? If he hadn't have pushed me over on the jetty, we wouldn't be in this mess. How do we know, Mombo, that you're not in league with Jethro against us and pretending to help us?"

"We don't know about Jethro, Summer, but I don't think Mombo is against us as he has looked after us so far and helped get you better after you were drugged."

Summer looked embarrassed, "I suppose you're right Roman, he has helped us all, but I'm worried it's all taking too long. We have lost touch with Axel and Daniel since we were put into this truck. They could be in danger for all we know. Also, what about the old man that went missing, what's happened to him?"

"Come on Summer, you are getting yourself all worked up, everything will be fine if you just trust me, and remain calm."

"Don't worry Summer, I will protect you. If Mombo tries to harm you, I will make sure he doesn't succeed."

Roman put his arm round Summer's shoulder's and gave her a reassuring hug.

"Thanks, Roman. I'll try to stay calm and stick to Mombo's plan."

Mombo gave them a reassuring smile and thanked them, reiterating for them to trust him.

The children settled down again and the atmosphere in the truck calmed a little. Mombo returned to his focus on the plan, whilst watching the progress of activity on the quayside, unaware that Axel and Daniel were making their way to where the ferry docked.

Out on the quay, Jethro was busy watching for the villains that had drugged Summer. Tom was with him, and they both scoured the crowds for the villains. They were hampered in their ability to pick them out, due to not having met them before or know what they looked like. They hoped that when Mombo brought the children to the ferry, the villains would make a play for them and when they did, they could step in and prevent them. They were unaware of the situation that had happened back on the mainland Miami to Arthur. Unaware also, that some of the children's parents were on their way to the island.

The villains, Max and Berni, on the other hand were anxious to carry out the bosses' commands. They were on their way to the quay side, having initially despatched two of their group to the old ferry that Tom owned. Having given them the instruction to prevent the ferry from leaving the island. This was to reduce the odds on missing the children when they got on a ferry. They were then to join Max and Berni at the main ferry port to help them there, to abduct the children and prevent them from leaving.

The two villains having carried out their task given by Max and Berni, were now on their way to the main ferry quay to join the others.

Mombo had highlighted Berni and Max to Jethro, but neither of them knew who the other two were, so it made it hard to identify them. Neither did they know what previous involvement they had had with Max and Berni, or if they were complete strangers to them as well. They didn't even know for sure if Max and Berni where the villains, or if they had been the ones to hurt Tom on his ferry. They just hoped that they had got it right.

23: THE PARENTS ARRIVE AT BIG BAHAMA FERRY PORT

Whilst Mombo and the others were waiting for the ferry to be ready for departure, the children's parents were due to arrive at the port. They had caught the ferry from Miami earlier that morning. Unlike the old one of Toms, their one was a modern vessel, built to withstand bad weather and carry a substantial amount of passengers and cars between the mainland and Bahama islands.

The ferry was in excellent condition, inside and out. It had good interior and exterior seating as well as a bar and restaurant. The vessel also travelled faster than Tom's and therefore this shortened the time of the journey. As it came into harbour, the little group discussed how they would try to find the children.

"Well Jean, where do you think they would be? I'm hoping they are at the quay waiting for a ferry to take them back to Miami."

"I just hope they are alright."

"Do you think we should alert the police, to make them aware we have arrived to take them home?"

"I'm not too sure about that Jean, after all we don't know if any of them are false, like the ones that Arthur came up against."

"Do you really think that's likely Tobias, after all it would be a bit risky for them in such a small place?"

"What do you reckon Stefan?"

"I am not sure, I suppose it's possible, although I think it would be better to inform the police just in case there are any problems finding them."

"Arthur, what do you think? Arthur! are you alright? You look like you've seen a ghost."

"Yes! Jean I'm fine. I just have a bad feeling about this trip and to top it all, I thought I just saw someone I recognised, over on the quay. I'm ok, I think my imagination is getting the better of me."

"Maybe you should have stayed behind at the hotel and got some rest. You have been through a lot over the last few days."

"Maybe you're right love, but I'm here now, besides if there are any bogus police here, I might recognise them before they can harm the children or us."

Still with a feeling of dread in the pit of his stomach, Arthur concentrated on listening to the others hatch a plan to find the children and take them back to the hotel. Arthur recalled what Daniel had said to him, about his bad feeling, when they told him of the holiday and what he described as his sixth sense. How they said it must be the shock of his mother's spontaneous action of booking the holiday, and his fear in regard to never having previously been on a plane or a really expensive holiday, either home or abroad.

Arthur regretted that they had been so flippant about his son's feelings. He could now understand what he had meant. He hoped that they had both been mistaken in their interpretation of their feeling. He hoped that the telepathy between them would be enough to keep them both safe. Well, there wasn't much he could do about it now, he told himself. He just needed to keep calm and focussed on ensuring that the children, as well as themselves, leave the island safely and return to the hotel on the mainland.

It's funny, he thought, all this hassle just because of an old man who lost his staff then went missing himself.

"Come on Arthur, stop your day-dreaming, the ferry has docked, and we need to disembark."

The ferry was quite crowded with passengers. Arthur took his wife's arm to help her. He feared that she may get jostled and hurt in the rush from people, who were in a hurry to get off the ferry. The quayside was very crowded. There were people clearing away debris from the storm. Others who were trying to sell their produce or wares. Queues were formed, of people waiting to embark onto the ferry due to leave for the mainland. Music, laughter, anger and bird chatter could be heard amongst the hustle and bustle.

Arthur scoured the crowds with his eyes but was unable to see the children.

"I can't see the children anywhere, can any of you?"

"No, not yet, but we need to keep alert in case they appear. It could be difficult to see them if they are separated or distributed amongst the crowds."

On checking that none of them had seen the children since disembarking, they all agreed to keep a lookout for them or anything or anyone that appeared suspicious.

24: THINGS HOT UP

Jethro and Tom were becoming impatient. They had been hanging around for hours with no sign of any people that they could definitely call villains. Even though Mombo had highlighted a few possibles, none of them had shown any behaviour of concern whilst they had been there.

Max and Berni were also waiting on the quayside. They were equally frustrated.

The other two guys that they had sent to stop Tom from using his ferry, had not yet returned to them. They were beginning to think the guys had done a bunk. If they didn't turn up soon, they would have to let the boss know. This would mean that they had failed to implement the boss's orders properly. The boss would be very angry and would probably refuse to pay them. Worse still, he may decide to do away with them permanently.

"Hey Berni, those guys we fetched with us this morning ain't come back yet. If they ain't here soon, I'm gonna send you to look for them, so I hope for their sake they get here soon."

"Yeah, well if they don't, I'm gonna waste em."

Whilst Max and Berni had been discussing what to do to the

two guys if they didn't return, they had not realised that they had crept up behind them and overheard the conversation.

"Oh yeah, who you gonna waste? You need to be careful what you're saying mate. What's to say me and him ain't gonna waste you?"

A distinct rift of distrust developed between them. Whilst this was all going on, time seemed to stand still.

The crowds became thicker, the heat was intolerable, and movement was restricted. A horn sounded to inform the people that the ferry was ready to take passengers.

On hearing the horn, Mombo got out of the truck and went around to the rear and opened the doors. "Okay you two, it's time for us to go. Stay close to me and keep an eye out for Jethro and Tom. They will be near the jetty and will safeguard you as you make your way onto it."

Roman and Summer got out of the truck.

"If anyone makes any attempt to harm you, they will grab them. If either of you recognise any of the villains, please tell us, then point them out."

"What do we do if they grab us and you are unable to grab them?"

"Do whatever you need to do to get away from them and run up the gangplank onto the ferry."

"What you mean kick them or bite them or something if we need to, if we have to get away?"

"What's going to happen to Axel and Daniel, how are they

going to get on the ferry, they are not even here?"

"Don't worry, I will go and fetch them as soon as I know you are safe. Come on both of you now, we need to hurry. Keep close to me as its very crowded, and the crowds could get ugly if they all make a rush for the ferry."

"I don't understand Mombo. Is it always so busy as this?"

"No Roman, it's because the storm has caused a lot of devastation and a lot of people want to get off the island. Some of them have lost everything. Don't forget that the other ferry is not in use either, so the people that would usually have gone from that quay have all converged on this one. The storm has calmed enough for some clearing up and the ferry to run, but there's nothing to say that the storm won't return later tonight. Well now, we are about fifteen feet from the ferry, do you think you could make your own way to it. You will see Jethro there and he will guide you on it. I will watch from here until you are safe aboard unless you appear in danger. In which case I will come to your aid. What say you?"

"Are you ready Summer? If so, I am too."

"Yes Roman, I'm ready. I can't wait to get back to the mainland and the hotel."

"I don't blame you, I think Daniel was right when he said it would end in trouble. Our adventure hasn't been much fun so far, has it?"

"Oh Roman, I'm so sorry. It was all my idea, I thought it would be such fun and we would find the !!!"

"Find the what?" said Mombo.

"Oh nothing, Mombo, just I thought we would find exploring the island exciting."

Roman looked from one to the other. He realised that Summer did not fully trust Mombo, although he had not done them any harm. In fact, he had only helped them so far.

"Okay Mombo we're ready to make our way to the ferry, please don't worry about us, we will be fine."

"Okay, be careful, stay close together, I shall watch you as best I can."

Summer and Roman joined hands and walked toward the ferry. After a few steps they turned and waved at Mombo, then turning back, set off at a sprint.

They had gone about halfway, having pushed and shoved people out of their way, when Summer saw Jethro.

"Come on Roman, Jethro's over there." She called and waved to him, in her excitement of seeing him, only to be grabbed from behind.

Her scream pierced Romans ears, and that of many people nearby. She struggled with her captor, kicking and screaming.

Roman turned to try and help her but he too was grabbed and dragged away from where she was standing.

Jethro having seen them, ran to her aid, only to be tripped up by Berni, who then pounced on him and held him down.

Summer continued screaming, as the crowds moved back in astonishment. Mombo pushed his way through the crowds to reach the children. As he did so he noticed a lady rushing to where Summer was grappling with her captor. As she reached the chaos that was unfolding in front of her, she grabbed the hair of the guy holding on to Summer.

"How dare you molest this young girl, you ruffian. Unhand her at once, or I'll make sure you regret your behaviour." The man loosened his grip on Summer and turned to face the lady, only to receive a loud hard slap across his face and the blow from a knee in his stomach.

A man had followed closely behind her, and as her captor had loosened his grip on Summer, he grabbed her and moved her away, she continued struggling, whilst, hysterical, sobbing loudly in between screams.

Jethro struggled to untangle himself from the tall guy who was pinning him down on the ground. He was being egged on by another guy, whilst Tom unsure what to do, stood by watching. He knew he didn't have the strength to help Jethro push the man off.

Bystanders watched in amazement as the chaos continued. Mombo had reached the children. He didn't recognise the man who had grabbed Summer, once the other man had loosened his grip on her. He wasn't sure if this man was a friend or another villain. Roman was still struggling with his captor. Mombo pushed his way in and pulled the guy off, of him. Roman, gasping for air having been punched in the stomach, fell to the ground. As he did so, Mombo saw another man come to his aid. He heard him say, "You're okay Roman. Just stay still for a minute, take some deep breaths. When you are ready, I'll help you up."

Roman gasped for air, then turning to the man, saying, "I don't understand, where did you come from? How did you find us?"

"Don't worry about that now son, let's get you out of this mess, before these guys start laying into you again."

"Oh! but we can't, we've got to help Summer, and wait for Axel and Daniel."

A scream came from Summer as he said this, and they both turned to see her being dragged by her hair out of the affray, by two men. One very tall, the other, short. They were dragging her across the quay away from the ferry dock toward a man who appeared to be part of the press. He was surrounded by cameramen and flashing lights, as they took pictures of the scene.

At that moment Mombo appeared, calling to Roman.

"Get back to the truck Roman, you will be safe there. I'll try and get Summer away from the men and bring her to the truck. Get back quickly before they grab you again"

Roman's rescuer looked from Roman to Mombo, and back again. "Do you know this man?"

"Yes, he has been helping us and brought us to the ferry this morning in his truck."

"Then do as he says. I will try to help him with rescuing Summer. What is his name?"

"His name is Mombo, he is a doctor and helped Summer get better and Daniel."

"What on earth has been going on Roman, how did you get into this mess?"

Roman was about to answer but was interrupted. “No, don’t tell me now, there’s not time, do as he said. I will go and help Mombo and you can tell me all about it later when everyone is safe. Now go!”

Roman raced off toward the truck, whilst Stefan ran off to follow Mombo in pursuit of Summer and her captors.

Jethro having been, knocked unconscious, was being tended to by, Tom and Jean.

Arthur and Tobias were still involved in fighting off the other two villains that had been enlisted by the boss. Arthur was beginning to tire as the guy got the upper hand on him and had him pinned to the ground. Tobias was battling to free Arthur and hold his assailant at the same time.

They were surprised suddenly, when their two assailants let out a yelp, and clutched their heads in pain. Loosening their grips on Arthur and Tobias, only to be lassoed with rope around their shoulders and dragged backward, causing them to lose their balance and fall.

Once on the ground they were jumped on and tied up with the rope, to prevent them from causing any more trouble. Arthur and Tobias watched in amazement whilst this was unfolding in front of them.

“Where did you two come from?”, asked Tobias.

“We were about to ask you the same?”

“What’s happened to Jethro? Is he going to be alright?”

"Who?"

"Jethro," Daniel pointed to where Jethro was laying.

"Oh him, do you know this guy, only I wasn't sure if he was trying to help or hinder us when he got cracked over the scull and slipped to the floor."

Jean looked up at Daniel. "He's going to be alright, but he will have a pretty big bump and nasty bruise on his head for a while. Does he live here? If so, do you know where, as I think he may need to be taken there? I don't think he will be walking any time soon."

"Mombo may know, he's a doctor and he asked Jethro to help him get us safely on to the ferry."

Tom stood beside Jethro. He turned to look at the boys when he heard their voices. "Where did you two come from? Does Mombo know you are here? Where did you get that stick from, that you're leaning on?"

"It's Axel's, he brought it with him. Why what's it to you?"

"Oh, nothing, no reason."

Jean and Arthur looked at the boys, relieved to see them, then looked at the two men that they had trussed up.

"Well, what we going to do with this lot?"

"Well, I suppose we will hand them over to the police and them deal with them."

"No, not yet Mum, let's wait for Mombo to come back and make sure Summer and Roman are safe."

"That's okay, but we can't just leave them here tied up. They will be trampled on by all these people."

"Why don't we take them over there behind the press, we can put them in the office and keep an eye on them."

"Okay Daniel, Tobias and I will take them across, whilst you, your Mum and Tom, help get Jethro over there too."

"Axel, can you come with us please?"

"If it's all the same to you sir, without wishing to be impolite, I would rather help with Jethro, as Daniel still has a bad ankle and needs the stick to help balance him. It would be better if he went with you, sir."

"What say you, Daniel?"

Daniel looked at his father then at Axel, and back to his father. He sensed that Axel was trying to tell him something but wasn't able to say it out loud.

"Axel's right Dad, I think he would be more help to Mum and Tom in getting Jethro across to the offices."

"That's settled then."

"Let's hurry, before things get nasty, these people have been held up enough and want to get on with their business."

"Axel, go and help the others with Jethro. Be careful with him though, he may be badly hurt."

"Daniel, you can clear the route through for us and we will bring these two guys along behind you. Let's be quick though, before they start struggling again."

As requested, Daniel led the way to where the press were standing and as he did so, he motioned to people for them to move out of his way. He led them through the group of reporters, but just as he was about to turn to his Dad and check it was far enough, he heard one of the two captives speak.

"Hey Boss, you gonna get these ropes off us, this little tike's bound us up in."

Daniel swung round to see who he was referring to as boss, dropping his hold on his stick as he did so. At first, he thought he was mistaken, however on regaining his balance, he bent to pick up his stick, just as the guy that was referred to as boss, stooped to do the same.

As the man picked up the stick and looked up toward Daniel, his face came closer to him. Daniel could see him clearly now and it confirmed to him that he was the person they had met at the Newspaper print offices.

He was about to thank him for picking up his stick, when the man said, "I'll take that, I wondered where it had gone, the old man must have spirited it away and given it to you or maybe you stole it."

Daniel could see that Jack did not recognise him, any more than the lady had, when they had seen her on the boat. Instead of saying who he was, he sensed that they were in danger, and leant forward and grabbed the stick.

"It is not yours, it belongs to my friend, and he has given it to me to help me balance as I have hurt my leg."

"This cannot be so, this is mine, you must have stolen it!" The man, Jack, held on to it but as he did so, Daniel became stronger, and was able to easily remove it from Jacks hand.

Jack looked in disbelief at his hand, after the stick was

removed. A clear burn line was embedded across his palm, where the stick had been. He was about to grab Daniel, when Arthur intervened, and moved Daniel out of the way.

Having also heard the two men refer to Jack as the boss, Arthur wanted an explanation as to why this was. The two men refused to say anything, other than that they wouldn't grass on anyone. Jack realised that things could get nasty, so just laughed them off saying they must be mad as he had never seen the guys before. They were still discussing this when Tom and Axel, appeared beside them.

"Hi Daniel, we are back." Axel then spoke quietly to Daniel, so that he couldn't be overheard. "We have put Jethro in the office and the guy is going to keep an eye on him until Mombo gets back. What's happening here, is there a problem?"

Keeping his voice low, Daniel replied "No Axel, its ok, these guys have just said that this man was their boss, but he had denied it. They are now saying they won't grass him up, so we can't be sure. The guy also said this stick belongs to him and that I must have stolen it. I told him that it belonged to a friend who had loaned it to me. I had to wrestle it off of him, but it was strange, because I swear the stick gave me the strength to do so. Not only that, but it left a burn mark on his hand, even though it wasn't hot."

"Do you recognise him Axel? Just nod or shake your head, I haven't told him who we are because I sense danger."

Axel turned and looked at the man, and quickly turned back to Daniel and nodded.

"Do you know where Mombo is or where he left his truck?

"No, why do you ask?"

"We need to find Roman, that's why, I figured he would be in Mombo's truck

"Do you know where Summer is Axel?"

"No, sorry Daniel, I wasn't watching where they went, did you not see her being dragged away?"

"Tom, did you see where they took Summer when they dragged her away?"

"Why yes, they dragged her over to the press people in front of the office, I didn't seem them after that."

"They must be near here then, surely they can't have got far. If they weren't in the office when you took Jethro there, they must have got her further away somehow. Maybe they had a car nearby, like Mombo?"

"Tom, do you know where Mombo parked his truck, we need to find Roman?"

"No not exactly, but he could see the office and quay from it, because he was watching for the villains and us from it. It must be ten or fifteen metres outside, because he was using binoculars.

25: THE HUNT IS ON

"Come on Axel, let's see if we can find them or Mombo's truck."

The two boys turned in the direction away from the quay and office and walked off, leaving Tom to explain where they had gone.

When Jean, Arthur and Tobias heard that the boys had gone off on their own again, Jean let out a sigh, "Now, we have lost them all again, so now what do we do?"

"Don't worry Jean, I'm sure we will find them again soon."

"That's all very well Arthur, but we don't know what they will get caught up in during the meantime. Who knows what danger lurks out there, after all, didn't they say that doctor guy had treated both Summer and Daniel?"

"Tom here reckons that they went off in that direction away from the quay, so maybe if we follow them, we can catch up with them."

"You could be right Tobias, what about it, Jean?"

"Okay Arthur, but someone needs to stay here in case they come back or one of the others do."

"That's okay Jean, if you and Tobias want to go, I will wait here. If Tom goes with you as well, he will recognise Mombo and be able to explain what's been happening."

"What about Jethro, shouldn't someone stay with him? After all he is in a bad way with concussion. I think maybe Tom should stay with him, as he knows him."

"There's no need for that Jean, as the office man is keeping an eye on him for us. Tom will be more use to us in his ability to recognise Mombo as we have not seen him or know him enough to recognise him ourselves."

"In that case we better hurry, or the trail will go cold and we won't find them."

Tobias, Jean and Tom soon departed and sped toward the direction that the children had gone. They didn't have far to go before they caught sight of Mombo's truck.

"That's it!"

"Are you sure?"

"Yes! I'm sure if you look inside, you should find the boy, Roman. Mombo told him to come back here and wait whilst he went to find the girl."

Tobias went forward and tried the back of the truck. It was empty, with no sign of Roman or the other two boys. There was no sign of Stefan or Mombo either.

"Oh! now what? So much for Roman being here, why do children never do what they are asked?"

"What worries me Tobias, is that he may have done, but someone has grabbed him since. We don't know how many villains are involved or even who they are."

"That's true Jean, but we must stay calm and hope that its child defiance rather than anything more sinister."

"Okay Tobias we're calm. Let's check out the truck a bit first to ensure there are no clues in there as to where the children may be. Tom, do you have any idea where Roman would have gone too?"

"No mister, I expect he has gone to find the girl. They seemed very close this morning."

"In that case he can't be far away, the guys dragged her off toward the press and the office. Let's see if we can track them down ourselves and get to the bottom of what's going on here."

Tobias closed the back of the truck and the three of them headed in the direction that they thought Roman would have taken.

Meanwhile, Daniel and Axel were also looking for Roman and Summer. They had also headed in the direction of the two villains that had taken Summer. Whilst they were walking, they tried to make sense of what had been happening when they arrived on the quay.

"Why do you think those guys were trying to grab Summer again. She is no use to them. She doesn't know anything?"

"Maybe they are worried that she will recognise them and tell the police."

"I heard the two guys call the bloke from the print, their boss. What's more, he didn't recognise, me or you, come to that. Not even when I dropped my stick. He tried to take it from me, it was strange, I held onto it and it gave me strength to resist him. He said it burnt his hand, but I think he must have done that beforehand. Don't you?"

"No Daniel, I know this is going to sound crazy, but I think the stick burnt his hand. I've been trying to tell you since we left the press building. When we were in there and you were talking to the man and lady, you may remember I was watching the print presses and the paper clippings that the staff were going through. On one of the front pages, there was an article about a missing old professor and the artefacts that had also disappeared. I'm sure it was the one you were looking for at the hotel the other day."

"But why didn't you say something then? Come to that why didn't he say something when we were there? He must have known and fobbed us off, by telling us the reporter was on holiday. I don't understand, why didn't the lady say something?"

"Probably Daniel, because he got angry and told her to get rid of us, maybe she is afraid of him."

"She didn't seem very afraid when we were on the yacht."

"You're right, but we probably didn't frighten her, because she laughed at us, remember?"

"Yeah, I hope she didn't hurt herself too much when she fell down the steps."

"Yeah, me too."

"Daniel, do you think the other hidden passenger could have been the old man?"

"I don't know, why do you ask?"

"Well, Mombo said that they were hiding out, and I don't know if you remember when you dropped your stick whilst we sat on the bench, I tried to show you something and you told me to stop it."

"Yes, what of it? What's that got to do with the old man?"

"I'm sure your stick was glowing when it lay on the floor and wonder if he was close. I think maybe your stick is one of his artefacts."

"If that's true, then how does Mombo fit in? She said he was their friend or at least the person who owned the yacht was."

"I don't know, maybe we will have to wait until we get back to the yacht to find out."

"In that case, we will have to be careful in case he is in league with the villains."

"I think if he was one of the villains, he wouldn't have helped us. I am not so sure about his wife though."

"Why's, that?"

"I don't know, it was just something about her, she cooked our food and I swear she put too many herbs in it or drugged us. You may not remember, but when we were all eating, we all started to feel really drowsy. Then they told us to lay down on the couch type bed. You all grew weaker. It was only when you held onto the stick that you grew stronger. I slept fitfully and overheard some of the conversation. I think Mombo suspects her as well. She was interested in the stick as well, so was Tom, do you think they are in league with Jethro?"

"I don't know, I always feel a sense of danger when he is around. In fact, I think we all do, but apart from that time he pushed Summer over on the jetty, he has been okay and helped us."

"Well Jethro is out of it at the moment. Tom has been injured as well and probably not strong enough to cause us a problem."

"Let's concentrate on finding Roman and Summer for now, then we can find Mombo. He may have gone back to his boat to look for us or check on his people that are hiding out."

"I think he went to find Summer, so I agree we need to do the same."

"Then let's go, we need to keep going in the direction they went in case they are hiding out somewhere."

The two boys quickened their pace, and instead of walking aimlessly, they looked into bushy areas, abandoned huts and cave areas, unaware that not far behind them, Jean, Tom and Tobias were following in their footsteps.

They had also found Mombo's truck, and no sign of Roman. Not knowing who, they could trust, they just continued to follow the trail that the men had taken with Summer.

Meanwhile Jean and Tobias were struggling to find Summer:

The people from the press had dispersed and a number of the crowds, that had been blocking their way, had reduced in size. They had left the quay behind, having walked the ten to fifteen yards to Mombo's truck, then continued in the same route line. The track was showing signs of storm damage. Tree branches were scattered about, huts were damaged, the roadside had abandoned cars, some badly damaged. The road was sandy in places, where the wind had swept it across the tarmac. Jean was determined to find the children and get them back to the hotel. The heat was unbearable with the damp atmosphere. She was angry with the children for going off, but even more angry, with the men who had attacked them all.

"We don't seem to be having any luck finding them. Do you think they would have doubled back, so that they can smuggle the kids off the island?"

"I suppose it's possible, what do you think Tom?"

"I dunno, but I reckon Mombo will go back to his truck some time, as he will need it to get back home."

"Let's go back then and see if Arthur has seen or heard anything. We can always look this way again later, if we need to."

Unaware that Daniel and Axel were up ahead, they turned around and retraced their steps to return to where they had left Arthur.

Meanwhile, Summer was once again bound and gagged, having been questioned numerous times by her captors.

"We need to let the boss man know that she is not telling us anything. She reckons she don't know what we are talking about."

"Okay I'm on it, you stay here with her, but make sure you don't hurt her. We may need to trade her for the others, so they don't spill the beans about the boss."

"Okay! Okay, I'll not touch her but hurry up I've had enough of her snivelling."

Max left Berni to watch Summer and disappeared through the

door in a hurry to find the boss. He didn't trust Berni and knew he would have to be quick, or Berni would run out of patience and take it out on Summer.

Max ran to where he knew the boss would be. The crowds had dispersed, so he didn't have to dodge too many people. He reached the boss some fifteen minutes later and gave him an update of what Summer was saying.

"Okay, get her back to the quay, we can use her to get those other two bungling idiots back, before they make bigger fools of themselves and grass us up. If they hadn't messed up by taking the wrong girl in the first place, we wouldn't be in this mess. Why you still standing there? You've got my instructions, so go!"

"Okay boss."

Max turned on his heel and retraced his steps back to where he had left Berni with Summer. When he got back however, he found Berni trussed up like a chicken, and no sign of Summer.

Unbeknown to him, two men had overheard them discussing their plan. They had watched Max leave the hiding place, then after waiting a while to check no one else was going to come out, they had crept in and overpowered Berni. It had taken both of them to wrestle him to the floor and tie him up. Then quickly untying, Summer, one of them picked her up and carried her out. The other one checked that Berni couldn't follow them and closed the door.

"Let's get her out of here.

"Okay, but we had better hurry, I'm not sure how long that guy will stay tied up. His friend could return any minute and set him free.

He looked a nasty piece of work, and I don't want to meet up with him again if I can help it.

Roman meanwhile was also hunting for Summer, but alas had not found her. He did, however, meet up with Axel and Daniel, who were trying to decide if they should search the boathouse or cave, where they had been when they first encountered the abductors.

"Hi you two! Where have you come from? I thought Mombo had you both stashed away somewhere safe?"

"He did, but we were worried about you two. We thought you may be in danger, so we decided to come out of hiding to help you."

"Do you know where they have taken Summer?"

"No, we were just trying to decide whether to look in the caves or the boathouse."

"Why don't we try the one that is closest to us here, if she's not there, we can then look in the other one."

"Roman, you are so clever sometimes, that's a great idea, why didn't we think of that?"

"Very funny! Ha Ha! Come on then let's try the boat house first."

The three boys raced to the boathouse. They stopped a few feet away and ducked down, then crept slowly to the building to see if anyone was inside.

There was no sound coming from inside, so they went in and checked it out, but no one was there.

"It looks like we're out of luck, we had better try the caves."

"Okay let's go."

Roman led the way, the route seemed to be etched in his brain from before. They checked them all, but still found no sign of them.

"Okay so where can they be?"

"Sorry Roman, I've no idea. What about you Axel?"

"Well, there's one place they could have taken her which no one would think of looking."

"Where's that then?"

"I know it sounds far-fetched, but if you think about it, then it makes sense. They could have taken her to the newspaper place."

"What? Why would they do that?"

"Sorry Roman, you don't know. Daniel and I went there after we left the yacht when we arrived on the island. The guy there who was called Jack, was unhappy about us being there and asking questions. The lady who was called Jane was much nicer and stopped him from being angry with us."

"Yes! Axel you're right, but when we last saw her, she was on Mombo's boat with someone else, as you know, they were hiding out there. I think they may have been hiding from him."

"Yes, you're right, but when we were in the newspaper offices print room, the paper was printing a lot of information about artefacts. I think he may have tried to kidnap the old guy who was a professor of archaeology."

"Yes! that's probably right Axel."

"Didn't you or someone say that those guys took Summer over to the press office when they grabbed her and as they were passing, they called Jack the boss man which he denied. If you remember, he said that the stick wasn't yours, but his, so he must have known where it came from."

"Well, I've heard enough, let's go and check it out."

Without any hesitation, the boys agreed with Roman and set off to check out the Newspaper print building to find Summer. On arrival however, they found the building shuttered tight, clearly not having been opened since the storm. Just to be sure, they circled the building checking for any gaps or small doors or windows either hidden or exposed, that would enable them to enter the building or peer through to look inside. This proved fruitless, and after about thirty minutes they concluded that it was a waste of time and needed to look somewhere else.

"But where can they have possibly taken her?"

"I don't know, maybe we should get back to the quay and see if anyone else has found her and taken her back there."

"Yes, perhaps you're right Roman, after all we were not the only ones looking for her."

"What do you think Axel?"

"I think Roman's right, if no one has found her, then maybe we can see if anyone else has any other ideas where to look."

"We had better hurry, we have been away for quite some time."

"You two go on ahead, don't wait for me, I'll slow, you up. I will follow on at a slower pace. Quick off you go!"

Roman and Axel raced on ahead as suggested by Daniel and were soon out of sight.

Meanwhile Mombo and Stefan had returned to Mombo's truck

only to find it empty. They had also searched as many places they could think of for Roman, but without success.

"Where to now sir?"

"We're not having much luck in finding Summer and seem to have lost Roman, so I think we need to go and check on the other two boys."

"Where are they then?"

"They are hidden away on my yacht with some other friends of mine. They should be quite safe, but it has been a long time since I left them, they will be wondering what's happening and why I hadn't returned sooner. Yes, I think it's best to go back to the yacht and explain. Maybe they will have some ideas of where to look next for Summer and Roman."

"Okay, so how do we get there?"

"We take the truck and drive there. It's not at the main quay, it's moored further round, nearer to the other quay. That's why I think they should be safe, as the others don't know where it is moored."

The two men agreed that Mombo should check on the boys. Stefan however decided it would be best for him to return to the others, as he needed to see if Roman or Summer had returned there. He thought the other parents would be wondering where he had gone.

26: ROUND IN CIRCLES

Mombo dropped Stefan off near to the quay and drove on to where his yacht was moored. He arrived at the place where he had moored his boat and looked around to see if he could see it. There had been a number of other small boats moored around it when he had last been on it. These seemed to have reduced in number, possibly due to the storm. Some may have been damaged and trawled away, some just moved by their owners who had need of them for their livelihood of fishing or water sports.

What he was surprised to find, was that not only had a number of small boats been moved, his own boat was not where he had left it.

He walked along the water's edge, looking for his yacht, but eventually had to accept it was no longer there.

Feeling confused and angry, he got back in his truck and drove along the track that led back toward the other quay, to see if his boat had slipped its mooring and drifted along with the tide. He was almost on top of the main quay where the ferry was, when he noticed his yacht, moored at the side of the quay, tucked in between some other motor yachts. He could not understand how this could have happened unless someone had physically sailed it there.

Anxious to know what had happened and if his passengers were still safe, he parked his truck and made his way over to the yacht.

After boarding, he called to Daniel and Axel but heard no reply. He went down below to check on the other two and found them both there.

The old man was asleep, but the lady was awake and pleased to see him. She told him what had happened. How the boys had been concerned for their friends and had sailed the boat round to the main ferry quay. They had arrived there that morning and they had left the yacht and not returned.

Mombo expressed his concern for the children and told the lady that he would go and look for them. He would, however, return later and arrange for them all to sail to the mainland and safety.

Disembarking from his yacht, he hurried back to his truck and drove to the ferry port.

Rather than park a distance from the port as before, this time he drove straight in and parked close to the main office.

He was relieved to see Stefan, who was standing talking to a couple of men and a lady. He went over to them and after introductions, he explained what had happened and that he was worried about Daniel and Axel, as they appeared to be missing.

Arthur and Tobias gave a look of astonishment, then laughed, "You say they sailed the yacht round the bay from one quay to the other? Well, I didn't know Daniel had it in him, I don't know about

Axel. So that's how they suddenly appeared on the quay when we were involved in that affray."

Mombo couldn't believe his ears, "You are telling me that you have seen them and that they were here earlier when those villains were apprehended?"

"Why yes, didn't you see them? Oh no, they didn't wait for you to get back but went off to find your truck and Roman."

"Let's hope they found him, because I didn't" said Mombo.

"We don't seem to be doing very well at finding the children. They are becoming more elusive than the villains have been."

"Perhaps we need to decide what to do next, after all we have captured some of the villains who are currently tied up in the ticket office. We also have Jethro injured and recovering in the back office, overseen by the ticket office man."

"Perhaps Jean, it would best for us all to stay here together and wait for the children to return here. They appear to be quite resourceful, and appear to know where to look, or at least find their way around. If they can't find Summer, I reckon they will come back here for help."

They were still discussing a possible plan when the boys interrupted them, by appearing alongside them.

"Hi, we're back, did anyone have any luck finding Summer, because we didn't?"

Arthur turned to see the boys when he heard Daniel's voice, "Sorry son, we haven't had any luck either. Perhaps we need to compare notes so we know where we have all looked and can work out where to look next. What do you reckon? "

"That's what we were thinking too, Dad."

"Let's all go over to the office area. There were a number of rooms there and maybe we can all discuss this together, in one of them. We can also check on Jethro and those villains whilst we are there."

"Sure Jean, that's a great idea, we can get some shelter there and maybe a drink of something.

They made their way across to the office area and found a room to sit in. The room was very shabby, its décor was dirty and stained. The chairs were stacked in a corner and a bench ran across the back of the room with a table stretched out in front of it.

"Sorry folks, it's not very comfortable but it will have to do, gather round the table and we will get started."

Well, as you can imagine, my mother had taken charge again. Her teacher training kicked in and overtook her feelings of fear and concern.

"Let's discuss where we have looked so far."

"Daniel, where did you and Axel go this morning?"

"We went to find Roman at Mombo's truck, then we looked in the caves and the boat house. Then when we couldn't find Summer, we went to look in the Newspaper building but it was shut up tight. All the shutters were still closed against the storm."

"Why did you go there?

"We were suspicious when we heard that the villains had called Jack their boss."

"Who is Jack?"

"Sorry Dad I forgot that none of you know, except maybe Mombo? He's the guy who works at the newspaper print office. Axel and I met him the day we arrived. There was a lady there with him also, who Mombo knows. We didn't know that then, we met her again on Mombo's boat."

Everyone turned to look at Mombo. "Sorry folks, I didn't know the kids had been to the newspaper office. Or that they had met the lady and Jack there."

"Daniel, why did you go there when you first came to the island?"

"Well Dad, we had split up into groups of two. We were trying to find out if anyone knew anything about the old man.

Summer and Roman had seen an old man having a row with a taxi driver and wondered if it could have been him. So, we, that's Axel and I, went to the newspaper office that was advertising a reward, to see if they knew anything. The other two were going to explore places on the island to see if they could find him.

Things got off to a bad start though, as Jethro seemed to push Summer over when she was getting off the ferry, but then he helped her up and later offered to take her and Roman round the island.

We went to the newspaper print offices and spoke to Jack and the lady, Jane. Jack was nice at first then seemed to get angry and made Jane get us to leave. Jane however was nice and spoke up for us. When we saw her on Mombo's boat however, she didn't recognise us.

She seemed different. Sort of moody, nice at first, then angry. She fell down the stairs when the boat lurched as the wave took it on the turn. I think she may have been hurt, but we couldn't see properly as it was dark.

We left them some food out so that they would find it if they needed it. Then left the boat when we docked at the quay."

Mombo confirmed that that he had been to the boat, and all was well there.

Jean asked for suggestions as to what they should do to find Summer. Arthur suggested that they split up. That he should see if he could find the two men who took Summer, and for Roman and Stefan to go with him. Axel, Mombo and Daniel to see if they could find the news paper man, to find out if he knew where Summer and the two guys were.

The others should stay put and keep an eye on Jethro and the two captured villains.

The others agreed, so they went their separate ways.

Mombo suggested that they use his truck to travel round the island, whilst seeking the whereabouts of Summer and her captors.

The boys agreed, as they were anxious to get back to the newspaper office in case the men had since returned there and opened the building up. Mombo, however, was or did not appear to be in such a hurry as he told them that he was going to drive home first.

The boys reluctantly agreed to this but questioned him as to why he felt it necessary.

When he explained that he was a doctor and may be needed. That his wife may have messages for him, they were more willing to. They were unaware that Mombo had another reason for visiting his wife first.

When they arrived there however, they found it deserted. There was no sign of his wife. Neither were there any messages for him. A basket of herbs lay on the table alongside bottles of potions. Cups stood on the side by the sink but nothing else seemed any different to when he had left that morning.

Mombo tried to hide his surprise at not finding his wife at home, by saying that she must have gone out to attend to an emergency in his absence.

The boys readily accepted this explanation and quickly returned to the truck.

Mombo turned the truck round and they headed toward the Newspaper office.

After stopping off at places that could possibly hide Summer from view, their impatience grew as they struggled to find her. On arrival at the Newspaper offices, they found it deserted. Feeling miserable and defeated, they decided to return to the quay and tell the others.

It was as they were making their way back to the truck, that Axel noticed a little hut that was almost hidden by undergrowth.

"Wait!" he whispered urgently, "Look, over there, can you see that place hidden amongst the trees?"

The other two looked toward where he was pointing and

confirmed they could. "Let's check it out. So that we are not seen, I suggest we keep low and move slowly on tiptoes."

Crouching they made their way through the undergrowth and crept up to the window area of the hut.

Sure enough, there were people in there. They could hear voices but were reluctant to look in through the window in case they were seen. Axel with his greater hearing ability, identified the voices of two men and one woman. They were talking about exchanging people, under orders, or be in trouble with the boss. He then heard the woman say that she would be glad to get rid of the snivelling kid.

Daniel guessed that they were holding Summer in there and that they were talking about going back to rescue their mates.

"We need to get back to the quay quickly and warn the others."

"Mombo is there a quicker route you can take, that avoids the storm damaged roads?"

"Yes, let's go, but stay low so they don't see you."

Daniel led the way, leaning heavy now on his stick, his back, leg and ankle aching. Soon they were back in the truck, heading back toward the quay.

Back at the quay:

Whilst Daniel, Axel and Mombo, had been busy exploring the little hut, activity had been taking place back at the quay. Jean, Tom and Tobias had been left there to keep an eye on the villains and Jethro. Tom and Tobias watched over the villains, whilst Jean administered care to Jethro in a separate room.

Jethro was gradually regaining conscious, but apart from a few unintelligible words, he was quiet. Jean, however, could hear the two men in the other room threatening to get their own back for being tied up. She heard Tom tell them to be quiet, or he would stick a piece of tape over their mouths.

"Yeah, you and whose army?" one of them replied.

They were still involved in this bating of each other when the door to the room swung open and a reporter entered.

"What's going on in here then? Why these guys tied up? Wait, let me get a photo of them."

Tobias tried to show the reporter the door and get him to leave, but the reporter was being very resistant. The two villains started making more fuss and threats, whilst the reported recorded it on camera.

Tobias grabbed his shoulder to turn him away, as he did so the reporter swung round and smashed him in the face with his camera. Tobias fell backwards and banged his head on the wall. Tom tried to break his fall but wasn't strong enough to stop him from falling.

The reporter bent to untie the two villains, but Tom pushed him to one side in an attempt to stop him. This however, only increased his anger, and he took a swing at Tom, who quickly ducked to miss it. He was about to retaliate but he stopped in his tracks as the man pulled out a gun.

Arthur, Stefan and Roman return to the quay offices:

Unaware of what had been happening, Arthur, Stefan and Roman returned to the quay offices, feeling frustrated and concerned about Summer, who was still missing.

Arthur went in to see Jean and report back their lack of progress. There was no sign of the ticket collector, so he assumed that Jean had told him she would take over and he could go about his business.

As he went into the office area, he sensed an atmosphere. The place seemed very quiet. He would have expected to have heard the others talking, yet he could hear nothing. He slowly opened the door to where he would expect to find the two men tied up, with someone keeping an eye on them.

Looking in he saw that the room was in total, disarray, the two men were no longer there. The ticket collector was tied up and Tobias lay on the floor in an unconscious state.

Arthur ran across to him, to check on how he was injured and get help. After checking that he was breathing, then having placed him in a recovery position, he left the room and went down the corridor to the one Jethro had been placed in. Still expecting to find Jean, he cautiously opened the door and went in.

Jethro was still there, as well as Jean. They were however tied up. Jethro lay propped up in the corner of the room. Jean was sat on a chair next to the desk, rope held her to the chair, and a man's checked handkerchief was tied round her mouth. On seeing Arthur, her eyes pleaded to him to untie her. Tears ran down her cheeks, both tears of sorrow and relief. Arthur ran across to her and untied her, then he went over to Jethro. Then returning to his wife he helped her out of the chair and hugged her to reassure her.

"Where is Tom?"

"I don't know, he went after the couple of guys that tied me up. Have you found, Summer?"

"No not yet. We have looked all over but with no luck. Have the others been back yet?"

"No, that is I don't think so, they haven't been in here since they left."

"How's Jethro been, has he come around and said anything? Did the guys come in here and say anything to him, or the other way around?"

"He heard the commotion when they barged in and tied me up. Tom was too quick for them and darted out of the room. Jethro sat up still dazed, one of the guys looked at him and said we will be back. Jethro didn't say anything. He passed out again soon after and hasn't said anything since he came around again."

"Well Jean, this is a fine mess, the villains have escaped. Tom's missing, both Jethro and Tobias have been injured and we still don't know where Summer is. Let's hope the others get back soon with some good news."

Meanwhile, Daniel, Mombo and Axel were equally anxious to meet up with the rest of the group. Aware now that the villains were hiding out in the hut, and that Summer, was likely to be held there, they were anxious to obtain help in freeing her.

They also wanted to warn the others that the villains were likely to try and cause more trouble, as in league with smugglers, they were, needing to trade one person for another, but they were not sure who they meant. If it wasn't Summer, then who else could it be? Daniel then remembered, the people on Mombo's boat. He wondered how much he could trust Mombo, could the woman in the hut be his wife. Could they be in league with the smugglers and involved in the kidnapping of the old man and Summer.

Daniel hoped that he had it wrong. After all, Mombo had helped them all, it didn't make sense for him to do that if he was involved in the kidnap plot. Yet something was amiss. There must be a ringleader, or the boss as they have heard him be called.

Is that Mombo, or Jack from the newspaper? Then again could it be Jethro, after all he was the one who pushed Summer on the quayside. Then does that mean Tom is also in league with Jethro and Mombo. If that's the case, how does Jack from the newspaper fit in? Daniel struggled to work it out, he hoped his thoughts would penetrate through to his father.

Mombo was also wondering what was happening and why he had heard his wife's voice coming from the people in the hut. He was concerned also that she spoke of a snivelling child.

Could she have meant, Summer? Could she really be in league with the villains? Surely, they are not trading Summer for Jethro. Is she in love with him and will go to any length to have him? No surely not, there must be some other explanation.

As he drove the children back to the quay, twisting in and out of rutted tracks and dodging fallen trees and branches, his mind remained in turmoil. What could be so important that these people could risk everything to obtain.

He knew that smuggling was rife on the island, but not kidnapping of children, this was something new. He vowed that he would get to the bottom of it, but first he must return to the others and seek their help.

Mombo and the boys arrive back at the Quay:

As they drew up at the quay, Daniel and Axel both sensed something was amiss. The quay was quiet, there was no sign of the ticket collector at the office window. Daniel sensed that his father was trying to warn him.

"Okay boys, we'll leave the truck here, it's not far to the office where we should find the others. With their help, it shouldn't be long before we can rescue Summer and get back to the mainland."

"Thanks, Mombo, let's hope they are able to tell us Summer's back and we don't need to worry anymore."

"I'm sorry Axel, but I don't think that's going to be the case. As you probably heard, the people in that hut were talking about a snivelling child, and that I would suggest they were referring to Summer."

"In that case, we must warn the others about the villains, and persuade them to help us to rescue Summer from them."

"Don't worry Axel. That's exactly what we are going to do".

Daniel:

They parked a short distance away from the office, so it took only minutes to reach our destination. Mombo, led the way, with Axel and me close behind. I was leaning heavily on my stick and supported by Axel, when we found the road potholed and broken.

Mombo went into the building first, he opened the first door where he expected to find the others. They were sitting waiting and hoping that the person or persons about to enter were friends, rather than enemies. They all thought, they had seen enough of villains for one day. A great sigh of relief was uttered as we walked in.

Jean was first to look up and see us.

"Thank goodness it's you three, is Summer not with you or Tom?"

"No Mum, we have not seen Tom, but we think we may know where Summer is, but we need your help to rescue her."

"Where?"

"There's a little hut, half hidden by bushes, at the back of the Newspaper building. We found it a short while ago. We came straight here. We crept up to it and although we couldn't see in through the windows, we could hear someone speaking. They were saying that they were going to trade somebody for someone else.

There was a woman there who said she was glad as she was fed up with the snivelling kid. We think they are going to come here and trade her for the villains or Jethro or someone."

"How soon do you think they will come? Did you recognise any of their voices? How many do you think there were?"

"It's difficult to say, maybe three or four, possibly more."

"Where is Jethro and the villains?"

"Jethro is in the other room, so is Tobias, both of whom have been injured. The villains are no longer here, they escaped."

"How did the villains escape from here?"

"A reporter came in, initially taking pictures, then he started undoing the ropes on the villains. Tobias and Tom tried to interrupt and stop him. He, however, took a swing at Tobias causing him to fall and bang his head. Tom managed to get away as the man pulled out a gun.

With Jethro and Tobias out of action and Tom having left the building, the reporter finished untying the villains and they left. The reporter chap told Jethro that he would be back."

"What did Jethro say to that?"

"Jethro didn't respond so we don't know if he knew the reporter or not."

"Thanks Mum. They may not come here but go to where Mombo's yacht was moored, if they are after the people he is hiding there."

"They probably won't know we moved it, unless Tom is in league with them. Perhaps we should split up, Axel and I can go to the yacht whilst Mombo can take you in his truck to the hut. That way we can warn the people on the boat and keep an eye on the people in the hut. Someone needs to stay here in case they turn up again"

"Tobias is injured so we need to count him out. Stefan could stay with Mum, whilst Roman and Dad could go with Mombo as they would recognise the villains. Summer would also recognise Roman which may be reassuring for her."

The plan agreed, we went our separate ways:

Axel and I left the office and headed toward the quay, then walked slowly to ensure that I could keep up. We looked back toward the offices and saw the others leave. As soon as the others disappeared in the opposite direction toward Mombo's truck, we doubled backed to the offices and hid from view. We were not sure but suspected that the kidnapper villains would appear soon.

If Jethro was part of their group, they wouldn't leave him for long. They wouldn't want him giving any information to the Police if they questioned him.

It wasn't long before we heard footsteps coming toward the offices. We waited out of sight in case it was just a traveller or innocent bystander. It was difficult to see clearly at first but after a few minutes, we crept round the side of the building and Axel recognised the voices he had heard at the hut. They burst into the building and demanded that Jethro be untied.

No one moved. The very tall guy picked up a chair to threaten everyone. My mother in her loud schoolteacher voice told him to put it down and not be stupid, if it wasn't, for the seriousness of the situation, it would have seemed funny. The little guy told his companion to do as he was told and instead of standing with his mouth open, to go and find Jethro and untie him.

The tall guy Berni, swung round and scowled at the short guy Max but left the room to do as he was bid. Max, then told them that they were taking Jethro, and to not try and stop them, or else.

Axel and I quickly slipped along and bolted the outside door, in an attempt, to stop or delay them from leaving. Jethro was still very groggy from the bang on his head.

There was no sign of Summer, so I figured that they were not planning on swapping her for Jethro. This meant that the other villains may be headed toward Mombo's yacht.

I signalled to Axel that we needed to go. He looked at me as if I was mad, so I signalled to him that I would explain on the way.

I figured that the others would find the hut deserted and return to the offices to regroup and in so doing would catch the villains with Jethro, before they could escape.

It meant that if the hut was deserted, time was of the essence to warn the couple who were hiding out on the yacht. With luck, they may have trouble finding the yacht as unaware that it had been moved from the other quay

This would give us extra time to reach the boat, warn the people and if necessary, get back to the quay offices to help the others. Moving the yacht was probably the best thing we had done, as it may protect the stowaways. I explained my thoughts to Axel as we went, fortunately, he agreed with me and willing to do as I suggested.

This was important to me, as I knew I couldn't manage without his help. If it wasn't for the odd shaped stick that he had found me, I would be on my knees as my foot was hurting badly. I was longing to just sit down for hours with my feet up but knowing this unlikely until I was back at the hotel, I struggled on.

27: BACK TO THE YACHT

It didn't take us too long to reach the yacht. I was hoping that the lady would be willing to listen to us. Axel climbed on board first then helped me on. The deck was deserted, so Axel called down to the cabin below. There was no response, so he climbed down to see if the people were still there and okay.

"Daniel, can you come down, there appears to be a problem down here. The lady and man that were hiding out seem to be asleep, but I can't wake them."

"Okay Axel, I'm coming, are you sure you can't wake them. "

"Be careful, yes, I'm sure."

I climbed down the stairs, taking great care not to fall. I held my stick in my mouth so that I could hold onto the rails with both hands.

I reached the bottom and looked over to where Axel was standing. The lady was asleep on the bench and looked very peaceful. The man, however, was much older than I was expecting. He was laying under the bench and half hidden by a blanket. He felt cold and clammy, I shook him to wake him, he stirred but did not wake. He reminded me of when we touched Summer in the cave. I guessed he had been drugged.

"Daniel, do you recognise him?"

"I don't know, it's very dark down here. Can we find a light switch or torch and then I can have a look at him?"

Axel found a switch and the cabin was flooded with light.

Sure enough, they were both in a very deep sleep, suggesting they had been drugged.

I clearly recognised the lady from the newspaper. Turning to look at the man, I removed the blanket to get a better view, I stepped back and just stared in disbelief.

"What is it Daniel? What's wrong, do you know who it is?"

Pulling myself together, I looked closer at the man. Sure, enough there was the long white beard, the lined face, twisted hands of an old man, I confirmed in my mind that it was the old man from the airport.

"It's him, Axel, it's the old man we came to the island to look for."

"Are you sure, what's he doing here? Is Mombo in league with the villains or does he try to protect him from them? If, so why is he drugged, would the lady have done that, if so, who drugged her?"

"I'm sorry Axel but I can't answer these questions, as I don't know. I think maybe we should try and make these two comfortable, if we can't bring them round. They seem cold so perhaps we should cover them in blankets and keep them warm. Perhaps there are some more in that chest over there."

Axel went over to the chest I was pointing to and opened it. It wasn't blankets he found.

"Look Daniel, this chest is full of old stuff, really old, like hundreds of years old."

To emphasise what he was saying he pulled out an old sword in its scabbard, various metal and pottery items of a bygone era, and coins.

"It looks like we have stumbled on somebody's treasure."

"Do you think that this is what it is all about? Do you think they are smugglers?"

"It makes sense, but why take an old man? That doesn't make sense."

We were still deliberating over it, when we heard footsteps on the upper deck.

"Quick, switch off the light Axel and hide behind the chest." I crouched down under the stairway.

Two men came down the stairway. They switched on the light and looked around the cabin. Peeking out at them, I realised that they were not the villains I had seen that morning. So, I surmised that they must be the sailors or smugglers that Mombo had used to help him stow Jane and the old man away. They were about to go over to the chest, but they heard the old man stir.

"I thought they were drugged to keep them quiet?"

"They were drugged but it must be wearing off."

"We better be quick if we are going to grab that treasure."

"Do you think that's wise, after all when the others get back, they will guess it was us?"

"We'll be miles away by then, after all they've got mixed up with those others and that bunch of kids. After all, we did what Mombo asked and smuggled these two over here and stowed them away. We can tell him that the stuff went over the side into the water during the storm."

"Go on then, grab it quick."

The two guys advanced toward the chest. I was afraid they would see Axel, however as they flung the lid of the chest open, Axel jumped up from behind it and grabbed the sword.

The guys jumped back in surprise, and as they did so I reached forward with the crooked stick and gave a sharp crack on the back of their legs, causing them to fall to their knees.

Axel then advanced with his sword pinning them down. Between us, we managed to prevent them from leaving. Axel removed the old rope that was round the chest and we tied them up.

Further sounds of awakening came from the drugged stowaways as we secured the two men. This was soon interrupted by the sound of footsteps from people climbing aboard the yacht. Once again, Axel and I hid and waited for the people to show themselves.

This time it was a lady that descended the steps into the cabin. We had turned off the lights, so it was difficult to see who she was. We then heard further footstep above, and a voice called down, "Is she there?"

The lady rummaged around in the dark, then shone a torch on Jane, "Yes, she's here, but she looks like she's asleep or drugged."

"Drat, now what?"

"Don't panic, I can give her something that will bring her round."

"Hurry up then, we need to get her out of there."

"We can replace her with the brat."

The lady moved Jane into a sitting position and injected her with a potion. After a few minutes, Jane started to come around. The lady put a gag in her mouth and tied her hands behind her back. Then supporting her, she made her climb the ladder, whilst she supported her from behind.

Axel and I remained hidden, as we didn't know who or how many people were up on deck.

A few minutes after they reached the top, a shuffling sound could be heard coming from above. Then a tall man descended the stairs with something over his shoulder, he looked like a fireman rescuing someone, however he wasn't, he was replacing the lady named Jane with another drugged female.

The tall man dumped his load onto the bench and returned to the upper deck. We waited until we heard them leave the yacht. We switched the light on again and looked at the body that the tall man had dumped. To our surprise and relief, it was Summer. Then our concern returned as she was drugged yet again. I covered her with a blanket to make her more comfortable, whilst we worked out a plan.

We now had the old man and Summer in one place, plus two of the villains but we needed to find the rest of the villains as well as our parents, and Mombo.

The only thing we could do was split up. I would stay on the yacht and prevent anyone coming down and trying to harm the old man or Summer. Axel would slip off the yacht and make his way back to the offices and tell the parents and try to persuade them and Roman to come to the yacht, whilst Axel went and contacted the police.

Having agreed our plan, Axel gave me the sword and told me to use it if in trouble. He then disappeared above and over the side of the yacht. Using his super speed ability, he ran to the ferry quay. He was just reaching the offices when he realised …. Well, I'll let him tell you himself.

Axel - Back At The Quay

Hi, I reached the quay and realised that when we had left there, we had been expecting the villains to turn up at the offices. The problem is, we didn't know how many of them that there were. We had two of them at the yacht tied up. We know two, at least, came onto the yacht and took Jane and replaced her with Summer. That made four. We know that one of the others may be Jethro or Jack, and we are not sure about Mombo either, or Tom. Come to that, where is Tom? He went off this morning and hasn't been seen since, unless he came back whilst Daniel and I were on the yacht. I suppose what I'm saying is, that I may be walking into a trap. Well so be it, I will just have to do my best to be brave.

Anyway, I should tell you that I'm not afraid, as there are lots of people around who can help. The quayside has become crowded since we left. There are people milling about, some with cases and rucksacks, others just with what they stand up in. I hadn't realised how much time had gone by. The next ferry was due to go out soon and there were a lot of people expecting to travel on it.

The weather is calm and sultry after the storm. Sweat is running down my back, possibly due to the heat but also my fear that everything could go wrong. I reached the offices and instead of going straight in, I crept around the perimeter, looking through windows and listening using my extra hearing sense. I was about to go into the entrance, when I saw Tom coming across from the direction of where Mombo's truck had been parked earlier. He saw me too, so I waved to him signalling him to keep quiet.

He came close and whispered, "Where's Jethro?"

"I don't know. He was in here when I left, but I don't know if he still is. Some guy threatened to come back and get him."

"What guy was that?"

"It was the reporter chap, you know the one who untied and took the two villains."

"We need to go in and see who is in there and if they are ok."

"I was just about to when I saw you, so maybe we can go in together now."

"Sure!"

Tom and I entered the offices, the ticket collector man was back at his desk and everything seemed calm. In a sense, too calm. We entered the first room and found it empty. The second room door was slightly ajar. I sensed an uneasy feeling. Tom however walked straight in. Jethro was gone. Jean, Tobias and Stefan were still there seated in a row. They were tied to their chairs, hands behind their backs with tape over their mouths. Arthur, Mombo and Roman were missing.

"Quick, help me untie them, there's not a moment to lose, we need to get to the hut and track Jethro and the rest of them down. If they are not there, they may be either at the newspaper office or on their way back to Mombo's yacht."

Once untied, they all started speaking at once. Comments like "Thank you!" "Wait until I get my hands on them!" "Let's get out of here."

"Stop chattering, there's no time, we need to find the others and get these villains to justice. Tom, do you think you could go and alert the island police and tell them what's been happening? We will need them to help us find and arrest the guys and help us get off this island."

"But what about Summer, where is she?"

"Don't worry about Summer, she is safe. We need to find Daniel's dad, Mombo and Roman."

We were still deliberating this when Arthur appeared, he told me that Roman and Mombo were at the hut. He had come back as he had sensed that Daniel had been trying to contact him through telepathy. He was sensing his family were in danger and telling him to get out of there.

"Tell me are there many people at the hut or have they split up and gone separate ways?"

"There's a woman there, with Jethro, she's administering to his needs. He is still groggy. There is a tall guy and short one, they brought Jethro back to the hut. They are the same two that pretended to be Officer Green and Officer Brown. They follow orders. The reporter chap and two other guys were there but have gone. I am not sure where. There was a lot of whispering going on between them which made it hard to hear them from outside the window."

"What are Mombo and Roman doing?"

"They are keeping an eye on the people in the hut. We didn't think they would go far whilst Jethro was groggy."

"Thank you, that's helpful to know, I am glad you came back. Tom and I will go to the hut with the police and then on to the Newspaper office and try to round them all up. I will ask Mombo to come back here with Roman and take you all to his yacht. We will meet you back there. You must be very quiet on the yacht as there are people there sleeping and if the villains escape and look for you there, they will hear you. You will find Daniel there he will explain what is happening."

I am glad to say that the others agreed to do as I suggested. It must have seemed odd having me, a child, telling adults what to do, but I was so concerned with getting the villains caught and back to the yacht, I never considered that I was overstepping the mark (that is being rude and arrogant). Tom and I went off to find the police and obtain their help and then seek out the others.

I have to say it was not an easy task. I wasn't too sure if Tom could be trusted. He hadn't said where he went after he left the affray that morning. He may be in league with the others. In addition, when we reached the Police hut, as it can't be described as much more than that, unlike our Police stations which are quite sturdy, brick-built buildings, this wasn't much more than a mud hut with a thatch roof and veranda that overlooked the sea. There were only a couple of officers available as most of their team were out helping to clear up the debris and disruption caused by the storm.

To them, a young boy requesting help to round up a group of villains, with no hard evidence to show them, they saw as laughable. It was then that Tom spoke up and explained the seriousness of the situation and reminded them that they would have had over the last few days, newspaper reports and tv reports expressing concern about missing children and a missing father as well as a missing professor.

He explained about the smuggling and the drug use and risk of international repercussions if they did not assist in bringing these people to justice.

The more senior of the, two Police officer, made some notes and then sent his colleague to bring back two more of the officers that were out. "I'm sorry sirs, the phone lines are down due to the storm."

Tom and I waited for them to return. It wasn't very long to wait, but to me it seemed like hours. The officer gave us a glass of water whilst we waited, as the heat of the day and the humidity brought beads of sweat to our bodies.

At last, the Policemen were ready to assist. Two of them were dispatched to the hut with instructions to arrest all on sight and bring them back to the station. We were to go with them and identify Mombo and Roman, so that they could be told to return to Mombo's yacht. We would then go on to the main newspaper building and arrest all those there. This seemed straight forward, as the hut was only a few feet from the main building but hidden from its view.

We set off at a good pace, the officers let me lead the way. They treated me with a modicum of respect to my face, although I thought they were uncertain if I was telling the truth.

Unfortunately, when we arrived at the hut there was no sign of Mombo or his truck, the people in the hut were also missing. The only one there was Roman, he lay on the floor of the hut, semi-conscious. Anxious to find out what had happened, I looked around for some water to bathe his face and bring him round. Tom however grabbed a bucket of rainwater from the doorway and poured some of it over Roman's face. It had the desired effect of bringing him round with a start, then he realised it was Tom and me, so relaxed.

"Where is everyone Roman, where's Mombo and the people that were in the hut?"

"Someone jumped us from behind while we were peeping through the window. We thought at first, Daniel's dad had come back but realised too late, that it wasn't him. They took us inside the hut, and when Mombo saw who was in there he was very cross and told them that they would be in trouble when the police arrived. The man that had jumped us had two others with him. He told them to tie us up. Jethro told them to leave me as I was just a kid, instead they could gag Mombo and he could drive them to his yacht. The police wouldn't look for them there, as they wouldn't expect a pillar of society to be involved with smugglers. They could take the stash there and sail it over to the mainland. Jethro told one of the guys to knock me out so that I don't go running to the police."

"Have you any idea how long ago they left?"

"Sorry Axel, I don't for certain, but I don't think it is very long, as I wasn't fully unconscious. I know, as I could hear them talking to each other about the drugs and other objects."

I turned to the Police officers and Tom, "We need to be quick if we are going to catch them. It sounds like the guys that were in the main building have taken Mombo and the others to the yacht as Jethro suggested. We better check first, then get to the Yacht ourselves."

"Officer, do you have any transport that we can use to get us there quickly?"

"We can pick up one of the police Land Rovers on route. You had better help your friend up, and we will check the other building. Then we will all make our way to the quay and find this yacht."

As expected, the main building was deserted, so we made our way back toward the quay. Noting the seriousness of the situation, the Police officers decided to call in extra help, or back up, as they describe it. When we picked up the Land Rover, they sent a message for more officers to meet us at the quay and to be armed just in case there was any funny business, as they put it.

As you can imagine, Roman and I found this all rather surreal. We felt as if we had fallen asleep and woke up, in some kind of movie.

We were put in the back of the police Land Rover and told to stay quiet and keep out of the way when we get back to the quay. I was asked to give directions to the yacht otherwise, to do as ordered.

It didn't take long by road, albeit a bit bumpy, and soon we were back on the quay and joined by four additional police officers. I pointed out the route to the yacht and the driver drove us to the yacht, the second Land Rover following on behind.

The police senior officer gave orders to the others, to stay back, and keep alert. He, with his colleague would follow myself and Roman onto the yacht, so as not to raise the suspicions of the villains if they should be on board.

As I climbed on to the yacht, I called to Daniel, that it was me and that I was back. I did not however get a response. I called again, saying that Roman was with me, and we had come aboard.

There was no one at the helm as the boat was docked. We cautiously made our way to the steps that led to the cabin below. Though it was quiet, with my extra hearing ability, I could pick up the sound of breathing coming from below. I signalled to Roman and the Police to stay at the top of the steps, and I made my way down. The area was in darkness, and as I adjusted my eyes, I sensed a movement behind me. As I went to switch on the light, the sound of a sword blade came slicing through the air. My instinct was to duck and cry out. "Who's there?" This time a horrendous laugh came as a reply. Then a "Who wants to know?" With, a sneer.

"It's Axel, where's, Daniel? What have you done to him?"

"Don't worry, you will get the same for meddling in our affairs. You and the rest of your meddling friends."

The sound of swishing noise came again, and as it came close, I dodged back just in time, as a crossbow dart whizzed past my ear.

I remembered the trunk of artefacts and treasure and realised someone must be using its contents to attack me with. I swung round and made for the light switch. Snapping it on it lit up the cabin. In the few seconds I had to see, who was in the cabin before my assailant switched it off, I noticed three people around the chest taking stuff out and putting it into large canvas sailor bags.

At the other end, Daniel, Summer, and the old man were huddled together with rope around them and gags in their mouths. Our parents were sat on bar stools with the tall man holding a gun over them. He had a leery menacing grin, which suggested it wouldn't take much for him to shoot them. As the light went off, I called for help as loud as I could, a shot rang out and I fell to the floor.

A huge commotion of police whistles, footsteps running across the boat floor above, screams, and more gunfire, was heard before the lights came on again. The passengers below deck, were shocked to find that our parents were no longer looking down the barrel of a gun.

Someone had, in the darkness, attacked the gun toting villain and brought him down. He lay on the floor, with blood and bruising to his forehead, blaspheming, with threats to get whoever had done it.

I, Axel, sat on the bottom step, looking and feeling dazed, the commotion had lasted but a few minutes, but its intensity had left me feeling shocked and bruised. The police from above had descended the stairs and were taking stock of the situation. The small cabin was cramped but our parents were no longer at the gunman's mercy. Daniel, Summer and the old man were still roped together.

I collected my thoughts and my wits about me and ran over to untie the others. The police officers were looking at the situation before them, scratching their heads, they looked as shocked as I had felt, to find so many people in such a small space.

The police officer whistled through his teeth, then with a look of shock and amazement uttered, "Well, I never, who have we got here?"

Roman slid quietly into the cabin. On seeing Summer, he ran to her to check she was okay. Tom had remained above on the deck with one of the officers.

Now that the lights were on, I realised that Mombo and Jethro and the other lady were not here, neither was the man from the newspaper. The three men I had seen were all in league together. The tall and short one, where the ones that had posed as detectives to abduct Arthur. The other two, were the two that their boss told them to find and help them waylay us children, to prevent us from catching the ferry home. Of course, I didn't know that then, it was only after the policeman asked who everyone was, that it became known.

Daniel explained things to the police officers and his Dad chipped in, well, why don't I let him tell you himself.

28: IN THE THICK OF IT – THE CAVALRY ARRIVE (that is the Police)

"Well officer, its rather a long story, and we have been cramped up down here for some time now. Would you object to us going up on deck before we tell you our story?"

"You can start lad, by telling me your names, then I'll let you go up one by one to wait on deck so that we can sort this mess out."

"Okay sir. My name is Daniel, this sir, is my father, Arthur and my mother Jean. This is an old man, possibly a professor, these here sir, are my friends Axel, Tobias and Stefan. Here are two other friends called Roman and Summer. The three men over there by that chest are villains, whose names I do not know, as is the one laying on the floor. From what I can see sir, there are some people that are missing who may present a danger to us. I think they may turn up at the yacht soon, not realising that we are all here."

"Right lad, you get this lot you call friends or family up on top. My man here will bring the villains up once they are all securely handcuffed."

"Thank you, officer."

I led the others up onto the deck, where I found a place to put them. Tom was up there with the officer. I explained to him what was happening, and that we still didn't know where Jethro, Mombo, the lady who had been on the yacht and Jack, also the lady who may or may not be Mombo's wife were, as they were not down below.

We were waiting for the police to bring up the villains, when a huge commotion erupted on the quayside. Mombo was ranting and raging at a lady that we later realised was his wife.

"How could you, do this"? he was saying. All he got was a laugh in return and a slap in the face. Holding onto his arms, preventing him from walking freely, were two men of Afro-Caribbean appearance. They, were followed by, a crowd of people who had heard the commotion. It was clear that they were unaware that we were on the yacht. I quickly told our group to slip down below, or make themselves invisible, so that if the new visitors decided to come on board, they would not see us. The police officer that had been with us had slipped down the stairs below to inform his senior of the situation.

The villains had been handcuffed, so they quickly gagged them, to prevent them raising an alarm, to warn the others. Then turned the lights off.

The treasure chest had been closed but the evidence of someone trying to loot it was laying on the floor. Canvas sailor bags and pieces of coinage and old pottery lay amongst them.

Hiding behind the trunk was a police officer, armed and ready to act if needed.

Mombo's voice drifted up to us, "This is all Jethro's doing isn't it. He's put you up to this hasn't he. Not satisfied with doing his smuggling with the likes of Tom, he had to draw you into his nasty little schemes?"

"Oh! you are pathetic. Do you think I would take orders from a whimp like Jethro? He hasn't the brain or the brawn to pull something off like this, let alone smuggle drugs and artefacts halfway across the world."

"Then who is it then? If it's not him, its surely not you? Don't tell me its Tom, as that would be laughable. He can't remember what day it is half the time, I'm surprised if he could make a living out of smuggling, let alone run some large gang of smugglers."

"You'll find out soon enough, in the meantime let's get aboard your yacht now that we have tracked it down. You thought you could fool us didn't you, by pretending you didn't know where it was?"

We heard the creaking of the moving stairway that they put alongside the yacht to enable them to climb aboard. Then came the sound of footsteps on the steps and eventually on the deck.

The conversation continued between Mombo and his wife. "Little did you know, but we retrieved the lady from here that you had stashed away and replaced her with that snivelling brat. If those kids hadn't messed things up by coming over here, asking awkward questions and poking their noses in, we would have had this all sorted by now. The stuff would be out of the country and no one the wiser."

"And what of the professor, where would he be now? Would

you have smuggled him out of the country too?"

"No! what would we want with some geriatric old fool. He's no use to us except for the reward for having found him, which luckily for you, we can now collect. What's more, we can tell the police that you abducted him. They will be so busy arresting you, they won't think to question us about the missing kids and artefacts treasure. They will take you away and lock you up, and with a bit of luck throw away the key."

"How could I have been so blind to not see how much you despised me and had little regard for our marriage and, reputation. You have me trussed up and therefore I am unable to do anything, so I suggest you go below and collect whatever you have stashed away. You can then leave my boat and follow your illicit lifestyle with your friends, but do not bother to return to our house, for you will not be welcome there. I shall have your belongings moved out. Go now and get your stash before I say something I regret."

With a high-pitched laugh, Mombo's wife and companions descended the steps into the cabin below.

"Quick you two, get some light in here and bag up the stuff out of the chest."

One of the men switched on a torch as they moved across the cabin to the chest. No sooner had they reached it and leant forward to pick up the sacks and lid of the chest, they were jumped on by the police officers that had been hiding in wait.

The light was snapped on and the room became enveloped by light and shadows. People seemed to crawl out of the woodwork in front and behind the captured villains.

The police, having overheard much of Mombo and his wife's conversation, were quite clear that they had good reason to arrest them.

The senior police officer turned to me, saying "Well master Daniel, we have collected a few more, maybe your friend Mombo can lead us to the rest."

"I hope so sir, as that poor old man and Summer have been through enough and we still don't know how Miss Jane fits into this and if she is alright."

"Well, my officers will ferry this lot back to the police hut for processing, then onto the pen (prison). We, however, will speak to Mombo and see if we can round up the rest and clear up this mess. I understand your parents are here. Is that correct?"

"Yes, sir."

"Then please bring them to me as I wish to talk with them about what they know of this situation."

My parents came across to him and my Mum explained: "We met the old man at the airport on arrival in America. He was in a state, saying someone had stolen his staff. He kept on collapsing on the floor and needed help. He went to a hotel, and we saw him again there as that was where we were booked into. He was arguing with the receptionist when we arrived, upset because she had given his room to someone else. It turned out that he was at the wrong hotel. We put him in a taxi to the Miami beach hotel and asked the receptionist to phone ahead and explain that he was on his way and needed a room and support straight away.

He had begged Daniel and my husband to go and visit him the next day to help him find his staff, so they did but when they got there, they were told that he hadn't checked in. Daniel and my husband were concerned about him but were unable to find him. The children then all went off together on the ferry, we thought just as an adventure outing and expected them to return for dinner that evening. They did not return and whilst us parents were having coffee together, two men claiming to be police officers, Detectives Green and Brown, came and arrested my husband and took him away and he did not return as expected. It appears he was beaten up because he wouldn't tell them where the old man was, he said he didn't know but they didn't believe him. They eventually received a phone call from someone they called the boss, who ordered them to let him go.

That is roughly all I know, except that the children have been here on the island ever since and we parents, got the ferry over to the island to try and find them and fetch them back to the mainland."

"So, you do not know this man who call himself Mombo, or his wife?"

"That is correct I do not know him and only heard about him today. I understand he helped the children for which I am grateful."

"Thank you, Ma'am, that has been very helpful, you may go, as can the other parents with you."

"Thank you."

The police officer, having cleared the yacht of prisoners and family members except for Daniel and his father, proceeded to go through his notes. He was surprised to find that he had arrested a number of smugglers and drug pushers in one day. That also, he was aware that there were kidnappers amongst them, as well as a ringleader still missing.

The only other adults on the yacht were one of his officers and the old man. He had kept him there, as he needed to question him but was unable to do so until the sedative had sufficiently worn off. Given that the man was elderly and apparently, highly strung, he had kept Daniel and his father back to act as a support for him.

The treasure chest had been removed to the police Land Rover, except for a few items that may be of use if they, are attacked by the remaining villains. These were a gold, fish shaped knife, a sabre and a crossbow. Each item was centuries old, and the police officer was reluctant to use them, but thought it was best to keep them back as a precaution.

"Okay master Daniel, who do you think is the ringleader and where do you think we will find him and the rest of the bad bunch?"

"Well officer, I heard the villains calling Jack, the Newspaper reporter the Boss Man, so I think it must be him. He also tried to take my stick off me claiming it was his. Axel managed to prevent it. If you need to know what he looks like, you may find it useful to get Axel to help you find him."

"What of the lady named Jane, you mentioned how does she fit into all this?"

"To be honest I am not sure, she was at the newspaper print when we went there. She was with Jack, but when he tried to get rid of us, she was nice and helpful. When we saw her on the yacht though she was with the old man, and when she came up the steps to the deck, she didn't recognise us at first. Her behaviour was very, changeable, she was nice one moment then angry. I don't know if she was protecting the old man for Mombo or whether she was keeping him prisoner for Jack. It seems that she is important, as they came and got her and brought Summer back in return. They must be in league with Jethro as well, because they collected him from the ticket offices."

"Well lad, you have been very helpful. I shall have a couple of my men go and find these villains. I will ask your father and Axel to accompany my officers to help them identify them. You are to stay here with me and the old man, so that we can question him, when he awakes."

True to his word the police officer despatched his officers to collect Axel and with the help of my father, seek out Jack, Jane and Jethro and anyone else they may have with them.

We waited and waited, the time passed slowly, we were just giving up on ever finding out why the old man had been abducted and who was involved in instigating such a plan, when the old man stirred. The drug was wearing off and he was coming around.

I fetched him a glass of water as well as a glass of brandy from the yacht's small mini bar. Having drank both, he became more focussed, grabbing me by the sleeve, insisting I help him.

We calmed him down, then the police officer asked some questions "Why did you come to America?"

"To give a lecture on archaeology."

"Who were you to meet here?"

"My daughter, the archaeologist."

"Why did you not register at your hotel?"

"Someone jumped me as I got out of my cab. Why are you asking me all these questions? Who are you, have you found my staff?"

The old man became agitated again, so we resettled him, but as we were going to resume questioning him, a ruckus could be heard on the deck above.

On mounting the steps, we found two police officers holding a handcuffed Jack, Jane and Jethro. The police officers were holding on to the men, whilst my father was holding onto Jane, who appeared unsteady on her feet. Jane was shown to a bench seat at the side of the yacht and an order was given for the old man to be brought up onto deck.

My father, having settled Jane onto the seat, went down and fetched the old man and put him on the seat alongside her.

The senior police officer observed them the whole time, trying to work out if there was a connection between them, or if indeed the lady was in league with the abductors. The old man, however, after a cursory look and smile at Jane, caught sight of Jack.

"What's he doing here?"

"Why do you know him?"

"Yes of course he drove the taxi, why is he here?"

"He is helping us with our enquiries."

"Do you know the lady that sits next to you?"

"Yes!"

"How do you know her?"

"She is a student of archaeology, and a very good one."

"Do you know why she is here with you?"

"To attend my lecture, what else?"

"Have you met before this trip to the Bahamas?"

"Yes, at my lectures and a dig."

The old man started to become agitated, and restless "Why are you asking me all these questions, have you found my staff?"

"Never mind that, sir. How came you to be on this yacht?"

"I don't know. I was in the taxi to the hotel and the next thing I know was on this yacht talking to you?"

"Do you know whose yacht it is?"

"No, why don't you?"

The police officer turned his attention back to Jane. "Can you tell me miss how you came to be on this yacht?"

"No officer, I don't. I was drugged and brought here by person or persons unknown?"

"Do you know who owns it?"

"No."

Daniel was about to interrupt the policeman, but Axel looked at him and shook his head, signing for him not to.

The policeman then turned his attention to Jack.

"Tell me Mr Jack, how did you come to be driving a taxi with this old man in it?"

"Someone ordered a taxi, there wasn't one available, so I was called as I help the taxi service out occasionally at weekends when they are extra busy."

"Why did you not take him to his hotel?"

I tried to, but he insisted he needed to go to a conference and told me to stop the cab, then he got out. We argued for a while, then he got back in the cab and I drove to the quay, where I dropped him. I then drove onto the ferry and returned to Bahama Island. And before you ask, no I haven't seen him since, until today."

The policeman then turned to Jethro.

"How do you fit into all this?"

"I'm sorry but I don't know what you mean. I met the children on the Bahama quay as they got off the boat. I was on my holiday, so I offered to take a couple round the island. We were unfortunately late back for the return ferry to the mainland, so I suggested that they try seeing if the old ferry man, Tom, could take them back to the mainland that night. I understand he agreed to take them on the morning of the next day."

"How do you know this man Jack and this lady Jane?"

"I'm sorry but I hadn't met them before today."

"Do you know whose boat this is?"

"Yes sir, it belongs to Mombo."

"So how do you know this Mombo?"

"I met his wife when I first came to the island, when I was

looking for a doctor. Mombo was away so she made me a potion to help with my queasy tummy. As I didn't know anyone else on the island, she showed me round and helped me find somewhere to stay. On my various visits back to the islands, I have looked her up and we have become friends. I have met Mombo a few times, he is a doctor and he has been at the house occasionally when I have visited. When he asked me to help him get the children safely back to the mainland, I agreed to help him. That's all!"

The police officer then asked for one of the police to be sent to collect Mombo.

In the meantime, he asked that those he had questioned remain on the yacht on the deck below.

As I went to get up, I slipped, and my stick flew out of my hand. Both the old man and Jack leant forward to retrieve it.

"That's my staff!" yelled the old man, as Jack picked it up.

"No, it's not old man, its mine."

"That's not true, Axel tell them!" I said, as I struggled to stand up.

The old man repeated over and over, "He stole my staff!"

"Be quiet old man," snapped Jack, "It's not yours, its mine."

Axel explained that he had found the staff whilst collecting wood to cook the fish. He recognised it straight away from pictures that he had seen in the newspaper reports when they were at the printers. The reports showed pictures and information of artefacts that had been dug up by the professor at his dig but had subsequently gone missing. One of these main artefacts was a staff with a wolf shaped head that had strange powers. When in the true hands of the owners, it would give them strength until all were reunited. Then it would shine a brilliant gold. When in the hands of a dishonest person, it would burn its mark into it.

Axel believed that by giving it to Daniel, it had given him strength to keep going when his tiredness and pain were upon him. He also believed that Jack had known about the value of the staff, and laid claim to it when he first saw Daniel using it.

The senior policeman turned to Jack. "Is this true?"

"No! it's all lies. These kids will say anything to get themselves out of trouble."

The police officer then turned to Axel, "Can you prove any of this?"

"Yes, ask Jack to show you the palm of his hand."

The police officer asked Jack "Let me see the palm of your hands."

Jack reluctantly complied. The officer checked them both and sure enough, there was a burn mark across one of them.

Jack snatched his hand back. "You can't prove a thing. I already had that burn. It still doesn't prove that it belongs to him or anyone else."

The police officer turned to Axel, "Do you have any other proof?"

"Yes sir, please ask Daniel to pass the stick to the old man."

"Daniel, you heard what your friend said, so please pass the stick to the professor."

I passed the stick to the old man, who I now know to be a professor of archaeology. As I did so, the feeling of strength went through me as he put his hand on it. Then the stick, known to him as a staff, started to glow and shine like bright gold. I felt a little unsteady on my feet, from the shock of what I saw, so I put my hand out to my father for support. As he took it to steady me, the staff stick shone brighter and brighter, the rich golden glow became almost dazzling. I dropped the stick from my hand and the glow dimmed a little. My father supported me still, whilst the old man professor held onto the staff. As he collapsed on the floor in shock, Jack grabbed the staff. Straight away it changed to a dirty grey colour and grew red as it burnt into his hand.

The police officer had watched it all his mouth open in amazement. Then gathering his wits about him, ordered his officer to handcuff Jack. He then asked Jane to take the staff from him. He watched closely to see what reaction the staff would have when she touched it, but it did not change, neither did it burn her, which if the myth was right, it meant that she was truthful.

"Do you have anything else to say Axel in regard to evidence?"

"Only that two men came to the boatshed and took a small dinghy to transport a lady and stow her alongside a hidden man in another boat ready to be taken to the mainland. The instructions given were to ensure the lady wasn't hurt, she was to be taken care of at least until whoever gave the order was ready for her."

"We don't know who hid the treasure down below in the cabin here, but some of the villains we caught seemed to know it was here and tried to take it. According to the newspaper report, the dig where the staff was obtained from, also included items such as the sabre and the small goldfish shaped knife, both of which also have special power. You may recall these items were laying on top of the chest earlier today alongside a crossbow, all of which would be valuable finds for smugglers. Arthur, Daniel's father knows who the two men were, that posed as Detective Green and Detective Brown, who claimed to be following orders. As regards to the others, I suggest you speak with Mombo who may be able to shed some light on how and why the professor and lady came to be on his yacht. Also, any involvement he is aware of by the rest of the people we have captured."

"Thank you for your help young man, I shall do just that. I will get my officers to take you and your friends to the quay offices so that you can be booked onto the next ferry and find some refreshment before you leave. Prior to you leaving, I would like you all to give a written statement to my officers."

After us all agreeing to do so, the senior police officer shook our hands then gave orders to his men.

The police officer arrested Jack and whilst all the others were hustled back down below, he was escorted back to the police hut.

29: THE CHILDREN AND PARENTS ARE TOLD THEY CAN CATCH THE NEXT FERRY TO MIAMI MAINLAND

After completing our written statements, we got ready to leave. I for one, was hungry and tired and I felt sure that the others would be also.

Mombo had not returned to the yacht, so no further progress had been made. The police were busy processing the villains. The senior policeman had given a number of orders and they were hopeful of completing a number of arrests that would clear up a lot of unsolved cases. It seems that we had stumbled onto a large scale, smuggling ring. Not only did they smuggle old relics and artefacts, they also smuggled drugs.

After a few quick instructions, the police Land Rovers were brought alongside the yacht. My father and I travelled in the one with the old professor man and Axel. Jane and Jethro travelled in the other one. The journey back to the quay offices was uneventful. The weather was sultry, a warm damp atmosphere that clung to your body. The road was rough from ruts caused by the storm therefore we were jostled about in the back of the Land Rover, creating a need at times to hold tight to the seat or anything that could support us.

We arrived at the quay in plenty of time for us to find something to eat, catch up with the others and discuss the day's events, before making necessary arrangements for travelling back on the next ferry to the mainland.

It all seemed like a dream as if nothing had really happened, that is until we were interrupted by Mombo, who was dragging a few guys behind him as well as his wife.

"Where's the police officers, I've a few more here for them to lock up and throw away the key. Including my dear sweet wife, who is in deep with the smugglers and drug pushers. Little did I know that behind my back, whilst I have been on the mainland, she has been helping to mastermind the smuggling of artefacts from the dig as well as a drug running business. Tom, Jethro, Jack, my wife and their cronies have been in league together. Jethro and Jack have been trying to use the children to track down the whereabouts of the professor. They sought to claim the reward as well as gain access to the treasure. My wife has been supplying them with drugs to enable them to keep them quiet. Tom was unwittingly drawn into their hideous plan when Jethro suggested to the children that he may be able to ferry them back to the mainland. By agreeing to take them and allowing them to stay in the boat house, he was tricked into providing a place where they could be found to enable the kidnap of Summer. Although I knew there was a plot to kidnap the professor, and therefore needed to intercept him on the way to the hotel, I was not aware that the taxi driver was Jack and that he was plotting to kidnap him. Jane was aware of the risk to the professor and his treasure, as she had overheard conversations between Jack and some of his cronies to try and smuggle the stuff to the mainland, but they needed access to it.

It was as a result of the call from the hotel for a taxi that alerted him to what had been happening at the airport. He was enraged when he found that I had intercepted and removed the professor before he could harm him. Instead, he put the advert in the paper and alerted Jethro, who was on the mainland, of the need to keep an eye on the people who had arrived at the airport at the same time as the professor. After watching the boy and his father go to the Miami Beach Hotel, he kept an eye on them. He was alerted to their interest in the professor again, when the children decided to catch the ferry. He was hoping they would lead them to the professor. That's why he latched onto Summer. When he realised that wasn't going to be, straight forward, he contacted Jack.

When Daniel and Axel turned up at the print offices, Jack became suspicious as they were asking questions. He thought they were trying to find the professor to claim the reward. He initiated the abduction of Arthur, Daniel's father, as he thought he may have knowledge of where he was being kept."

"I don't understand Mombo. How came you to have the Professor and Jane, hidden on your yacht?"

"The Miami Police have been watching the smuggling ring for some time but being unable to identify the whole gang prevented them from acting on arrests. I have known the professor and Jane for a long time. Jane is not only a student of his, but she is also his daughter. We met, when the dig the professor was working on, came across a skeleton. I was called in as the police surgeon/pathologist specialist. Since then, I have worked on a number of cases with the professor and Jane. It was Jane that alerted us to the smuggling ring.

Given the state that the professor was in when he arrived at the airport and the subsequent hotel, it became clear to me that I would need the help of Jane to keep him sedated and settled in my yacht. At first, she was angry, not believing that Jack was involved, as she had known him to be involved in smuggling stuff but not kidnap. It was necessary, therefore, to sedate her for a while until we could move her to the yacht as well. Hopefully, when the police have rounded up the whole gang, we will be able to reinstate Jane at the Print and the Professor at his university on the mainland. Where are the police? These guys here are tied up however they need transporting to the cells and processing."

"I'm sorry Mombo, they are not here. The Police chief arranged for us to come back here to arrange our bookings for return by ferry to the mainland. Once we were dropped off, the police returned to the Police hut and the chief was on your yacht waiting for you."

"I don't understand, I have just come from my yacht. It was deserted, even the chest of treasure was removed. There was no sign that anyone had ever been there. I was surprised to find that no one was doing forensic tests. They must have cleared everything out pretty quick."

"There must be some mistake, are you sure they haven't just moved it to a different part of the yacht?"

"No, I checked, it is all cleared out."

"Have you been to the Police hut?"

"No, I came straight here, as I thought the Police chief at least would be here?"

"Well, he definitely said he wishes to speak to you, so perhaps after he finished at your yacht, maybe he returned to the Police hut."

"Thank you, Daniel, I'll make my way over there. I should have done that before coming here, how silly of me. Well, thank you for all your help, have a good journey home."

With that he got in his truck and drove away. Assuming that all was in order and Mombo with his prisoners, would find the Police chief at the Police hut, we all collected our things and made our way to the quay and waited at the queue for the ferry. You can imagine my surprise when I saw the Police chief loading the treasure chest onto the ferry. What was worse, his officers were also loading the prisoners onto the ferry. I knew they could do us no harm as they were handcuffed, yet that sense of danger came over me.

We were just climbing the gangplank to board the ferry, when Mombo turned up. He seemed somewhat flustered, "Where is he?"

"Who?"

"The police chief, I've looked everywhere for him."

"Why? He's loading the chest and prisoners onto the ferry near the rear of the boat."

Without answering he went off in search of him.

We had just boarded, when we heard loud voices in argument. Mombo and the chief were in dispute about the transfer of the treasure to the mainland.

The villains Mombo brought, had been loaded and the police officers had left the quay except for the chief, who was to travel with the treasure and villains to the mainland to arrange for them to be transferred into Miami police custody.

We at last set sail on our homeward journey, and we sat back to relax, aware that the journey took about two hours minimum.

Tired and dishevelled, we chatted about the previous couple of days and how exciting it had been, bringing to justice a large smuggling ring or two.

The ferry was full, many people escaping the island due to the storm having destroyed their homes or possessions. The rumour that there may be treasure on board, created a tense atmosphere and the risk of violence, so we kept our voices low.

As it turned out, the journey continued uneventful and after a few hours we were disembarked on the Miami quay.

My mother once again took charge and arranged for our stuff to be taken to a taxi. Then she turned to the old man and Jane and informed them that if the room was no longer available at the Miami Beach hotel, then she would arrange for them to stay at the Miami hotel. Then she told their taxi driver to take the two of them to their hotel and to make sure they were booked in before leaving.

It was a strange sight that presented itself in the foyer of the

Miami Hotel that late afternoon, a group of dishevelled adults and their dirty dishevelled children.

30: BACK AT THE HOTEL MIAMI

On receipt of our room keys, we separated and found our rooms, having ordered a pot of coffee for everyone and some coca cola. Hot baths and a nap were the order of the day, these to be followed by the evening meal.

Discussion was minimal until we all reconvened in the dining room. There we met up with the others and after giving our orders for food, we fell into discussion about the events over the previous few days.

Tired and well fed, we finished our meals and made our way to our rooms. An early night was welcomed by all, and we fell into our beds.

The next day brought sunshine and everyone looked forward to the remaining days of our holiday. We had been promised a trip to a theme park and adventure island, so our thoughts were distracted from what we had all been through on Bahama Island. In a sense, it was an anti-climax to something that had seemed surreal, exciting and frightening, but we were all in a hurry to put it behind us for a while and have some good plain fun.

It was a few days later that we saw a report in the Miami

newspaper that praised the Bahama police for rounding up both smuggling rings. A drug smuggling ring, as well as a historic relics and antiques one. The report included information about a few artefacts that had been recovered, but there was no mention of a large chest of treasure.

The report went on to say that the professor had been found and was reinstated at his holiday residence and would be returning to his university following the summer recess period. A substantial reward had been offered for his safe return and would be passed on to the appropriate person or persons. In the interests of safety, no details of whom would be divulged.

"It's odd, Axel, there is no mention of Mombo or the treasure chest that was loaded onto the ferry. It's as if it didn't exist, do you think they could have kept it, the police I mean?"

"Maybe that's what Mombo and the police chief was arguing about at the ferry port. Perhaps they had to give it back to him, after all it had been on his yacht and may have been his."

"Why yes, I suppose that's possible, after all he was hiding the professor and his daughter, and maybe it was theirs and not meant to be taken by the police."

"Yes, you're probably right, which is why Mombo was trying to protect it, when he had it transported to his yacht. Besides, I think there is a stranger mystery that I don't understand, Daniel."

"Really, what's that?"

"Why the staff that I gave you, shone bright gold when you, your father and the old man all held on to it."

"I wish I knew the answer to that myself, maybe my father can shed some light on it. In the meantime, let's forget about it all and go for a swim, that sea looks really inviting."

"Okay, I'll race you to the water, last one in buys the ice cream."

The rest of the day was spent swimming and our holiday continued in the same vein. The last day came and we all wished it could be longer. That, unfortunately, wasn't possible and as we packed ready to go home to our respective houses, we agreed that we had all enjoyed everybody's company and would like to meet up again.

It was with this thought in mind, our holidays over, that we separated and caught our respective planes.

31: EPILOGUE

I knew it would end in trouble!

Having returned home some twelve hours later, it was like coming down to earth with a bump. Not that the landing was bad or anything, but when alighting from the plane we were met with gusty wind and rain. Gone was the hot sunshine of the holiday in America, the ability to walk round in shorts and, shirt sleeves. It was a rapid change to overcoats and stout shoes or be drenched before you reach the baggage stand.

We were back and normal life would resume, or at least that was what we expected to happen. At first, my main thought was to catch up with my friends, so I contacted them, and we all met up. We were expecting to start back at school in a few days but thought maybe we could go to the cinema for the afternoon. Of course, when I say friends, I mean the ones I have in England, not the ones I met on holiday.

It was good to meet with them and the film was good, so was the popcorn and coke. For all the time I had spent in the States, I don't think I'd enjoyed myself so much, probably because of all the pressure we were under over there to do so.

It's hard, having a holiday when you know people are after you. When your new friends are being kidnapped or drugged. When you've been in a fight or knocked out. Coming home was luxury that at one time my friends and I thought we would never be able to do.

Now that I'm back, and Summer, Axel and Roman had returned safely to their respective homes, it was now time to return to our normal daily school and work routine.

The next couple of days went very quickly, and soon school was the main agenda. Mum had ensured my uniform was crisp and clean with all the necessary name labels intact. With her being a teacher, I had to be presentable so as not to cause any embarrassment to her. I didn't mind having a teacher for a Mum, but sometimes I did wonder if I would ever come up to her expectations. My Dad returned to work also, and normal life resumed for the next few weeks.

It was a Saturday morning when Dad received a letter from America. Thinking it was from one of the people we had met there, he opened it straight away whilst we had breakfast. Well, his colour drained from his face and his jaw dropped.

"What is it dear, you look dreadful, is it, bad news?"

"Sorry dear, can you excuse me?" And he hurriedly removed himself from the table, causing his chair to go over backwards. He returned over an hour later, having spent the time in his study reading the letter through a number of times, before making some phone calls.

The letter had come from Jane, of the Bahama times. She had written on behalf of the Old Professor:

Dear Arthur,

I trust your journey home from Miami was enjoyable and uneventful, and that you are all in good health. My father, the professor has asked me to pass on to you his thanks for your help and support whilst in Miami and the Bahama's.

His health is unfortunately not good therefore he is anxious to pass on some important information to you before it is too late. I enclose a copy of our family tree and have circled the ones that you need to take a close look at. You may recall that following his accident, your son, Daniel was, supported, by a stick. This stick was indeed the staff that my father had thought stolen when at the airport. We do not believe your son or any of his friends or their parents stole it. We realise that the smugglers must have dropped it when they were transporting their find.

The staff has had special significance in our family for many years, even centuries. It is the object that can only be safely held by a family member. It is those family members that are able to release its powers, and when combined together, its full power is brought into effect, and it shines pure gold.

You may remember that when my father, yourself and your son, Daniel all held onto it at once, the staff began to glow and eventually shone a brilliant gold. This is because our family, through the ages, have been blessed with special powers.

Unfortunately, the staff can also cause harm, as it did so in the case of

Jack when he tried to lay claim to it. I expect this is all a bit of a shock to you and probably sounds far-fetched, but the truth is you were placed for adoption following birth for your safety, due to the fears of people that the power may be used against them.

My father never expected to meet up with his son ever again and was overwhelmed when he realised what had happened. He is anxious for you to know that he has always loved you and wishes you to know you have a sister. He is proud to have met your son, who he felt a connection with straight away. He has sent your son a small gift, which he hopes he will treasure throughout his life.

I hope you can find it in your heart to forgive your father for his actions at your birth and maybe visit us one day in the not-too-distant future.

Yours sincerely

Your sister

Jane

Well, when my father read it out to us, both my mother and I were stunned. Straight away I remembered the feeling of the old man's eyes boring into my back and his thoughts running through my head. The strange feeling of strength that came to me each time, as soon as I picked up the staff.

I was intrigued that Jane had mentioned he was sending me a gift, and I started wondering what that could be. As any typical boy, this became more interesting to me than the other contents of the letter. I pestered my Mum and Dad to let me know as soon as it arrived. This, unfortunately, didn't happen for a least another five days. I came home from school and my mother was staying late in her class. My Dad was still at work, so I got on with my homework. I was just getting to the end of it when the doorbell rang. It was a neighbour apologising for disturbing me but holding out a package that had been delivered to them by mistake.

I took the package and thanked her. After closing the door, I turned the package over and saw that it was addressed to me. I knew I should wait until my parents arrived home before opening it, however curiosity got the better of me. It wasn't a very big package, but it was oblong in shape. Sealed with lots of tape and an American stamp to indicate where it had come from.

I ripped open the package and dropped its contents onto the table and in my astonishment at its contents. I just stood and stared at it. I was still staring at it when my Mum came in.

"What's that Daniel?"

I showed her the packaging and whispered, "It's the fish shaped knife. The one that was amongst the treasure from the dig."

"Let me have a look at it while you see if there is a note in the package." I picked up the knife and as I did so, it started to glow, at least I thought it did, but my Mum said it was probably just a trick of the light. When I gave it to her the glow disappeared the knife just had a dull gold appearance. There was a note, which just said, *Keep it safe and it will keep you safe, signed from a grateful old man and his daughter.*

"Can I keep it Mum?"

"Check with your Dad when he gets home. If he is okay with it, then yes."

It seemed an age before my father returned, but I'm pleased to say that when he saw it, he agreed to me keeping it. I noticed the glow again when he picked it up and turned it over in his hand. He looked at me and I smiled and acknowledged his unasked question that it had glowed for me too.

We sat down for dinner that night wondering what would happen next. It was a few days later that we were able to stop wondering. An official letter arrived addressed to my father from the State Police in Miami.

Air flight tickets were enclosed and a request for my father to attend court to give evidence about the people that had abducted him from the hotel, whilst we were on holiday there. Although it was a request, it was written in such a way that if he was to refuse, then they would apply for a court order to make him attend. The plane tickets were dated one week in advance of his receipt of the letter.

Once again, I had those feelings of anxiety and thoughts that it would all end in trouble.

I need not have worried, as Dad received a telegram the day of the flight to say it had been cancelled. The case had been dealt with and his evidence was no longer required, as the villains had admitted the offence.

I have to say we all felt a sense of relief, we agreed that our next holiday would be as far away from Miami and the Bahamas as possible.

So, without wishing to say I told you so. I was right when I said we would end up in trouble. I have to say though, although I had not wanted to go, and sounded to myself like an ungrateful child, with lots of unfounded misgivings, although they proved to be right, I have to say I am glad I went, as I had a great adventure and made some brilliant new friends.

I can't wait until our next holiday, as our parents have agreed that we can all meet up again at our next summer holiday destination, provided we don't get into any mischief. As to which of course we said we wouldn't. So, if you want to know what mischief we didn't get up to, then watch this space!

ABOUT THE AUTHOR

This is a first Novel.

This story is complete fiction, or at least that's what I tell myself.

It all started when I was asked to make up a bedtime story. To accommodate this request, I started to trail through my memory. I recalled a holiday that had happened many years before which I thought would be a good starting point. Given that the recipient was due to embark on a first long-haul plane flight to a foreign country. I remembered having mixed emotions about my first long plane flight to America, not that their destination was the same.

Daily additions to the story would be told at night over the weeks to come with discussions about possible ideas for a plot

Until eventually it was written down, at the recipient's request, to hopefully one day be published as a book.

Printed in Great Britain
by Amazon

80129129R00161